Project BTB

E. G. Ross

What genius single-handedly conceived the superweapon for World War Three? How far will the government go to control him? What can he do to save his sanity, freedom and the woman he loves?

In *Project BTB*, E. G. Ross plunges us into the sec-ret side of his previous thriller, *Engels Extension*, and introduces an extraordinary new hero. *Project BTB* spans three decades with intense intrigue and eerie, emerging technology.

PROJECT BTB

Expanded Print Edition

Part One:
LOST IN THE CAVES

Part Two:
THE REVELATION

E. G. ROSS

PREMIERE EDITIONS INTERNATIONAL, INC.
CORVALLIS, OREGON

Portions of *Project BTB* were previously released in condensed audio editions as Commuter Books^{SM} with these titles:

> *Before the Beginning: Lost in the Caves*
> *Before the Beginning: The Revelation*

Also in this series by E. G. Ross:
> *Engels Extension*

Published by:
Premiere Editions International, Inc.
2397 N.W. Kings Blvd. #311
Corvallis OR 97330

Telephone: (541) 752-4239
FAX: (541) 752-4463

Internet Web Site:
www.premiere-editions.com

Editors: Irene L. Gresick and Beatrice Stauss
Graphic Designer: René L. Redelsperger
Cover Photography: Bill Lioio

ISBN: 1-891519-24-7
Library of Congress Card Number:
00-101503
Printed in the United States of America
Cascade Printing Company, Corvallis OR

DEDICATION:

To strategist Tu Yu, who two millennia ago observed, "When a cat is at the rathole, ten thousand rats dare not come out."

ACKNOWLEDGMENTS:

Susan A. Peterson for her first-there insights and encouragement; Irene Gresick and staff at Premiere Editions International for their continued confidence; and my loyal contacts in the defense and technology communities.

Part One:

LOST IN THE CAVES

Chapter 1

Everything has a reason. If you persist, you can find it. I try to remember that. I know it's true. I just don't always understand how to make it work — at least not right away. It takes practice, I guess. Patience, too, because life can test your trust in reason. Can it ever! Take this weird business with Darkhorse.

How was I to know way back then that I'd stumbled into what became World War 3, into what the historians sometimes call the Engels Extension Conflict? How was I to know that I'd help cause that war? Me, a stupid teenage kid! How was I to know that an out of the way town was the secret base for some of the oddest—

Well, just a minute now. I'm getting ahead of myself. Let me calm down and start at the beginning. My name is— Uh, no, that doesn't matter. Not yet. Probably best that you don't know for awhile. That no one knows.

Let's see, then. Where do I start? With Dan, I suppose. It always seems to come back to him.

I don't remember how my cousin Dan and I first discovered my half of the caves. Maybe it'll come to me as I start to tell it. I hope so. It seems that I ought to be able to remember more. However, as Dan used to say, the difference between "ought" and "can" is sometimes a canyon. The simple explanation is that subsequent events overshadowed the discovery; dampened my recollections. They say traumatic events can do that. Lately I try not to consider it too intensely. I'm afraid that if I got started on it again some Saturday morning after one too many beers during the all-night Friday poker game, I might be tempted to tromp up to Darkhorse Butte and take a look in my half of the caves once more.

No matter how waxed I got, Dan couldn't go with me. Not anymore. I haven't seen Dan in — what's it been? Thirty years? Yeah, about that. Been awhile. Common sense tells me I'll never see him again. I hope, though. Because everything has a reason. Dan used to pound that into me. Reason wins, he said, even if it doesn't seem like it at the time.

Guess I'd better step back. Explain a few things.

I'm an ordinary guy with a cheap digital recorder. I'm trying to make sense of what happened to me. That's why I'm recording this on my own, secretly, because — well, because I have to get it out there somehow, soon. I don't have a lot of time. They're after me, you see, and that means —

Well, never mind about *that*. Later on that.

Okay, when I said "my half of the caves," I put it that way on purpose. There's a lot I don't remember clearly, but some things stand out. I know for sure that my caves are up there in old Darkhorse Butte. I truly don't recall where Dan's caves are anymore. Not exactly. The psychologists would call it a mental block. If I got put under hypnosis or shot up with one of the new drugs or zapped with a virtual therapy program, maybe I'd be able to remember more than that Dan's caves were near his old farm somewhere by Salem, Oregon. That's about forty miles up the Willamette Valley. Darkhorse Butte, where my caves are, is due west of my old home town of Lebanon. That's where I live again. I do and I don't. Later on that, too.

If you're not familiar with the Willamette Valley, merely by looking at the heavy blanket of flora— the fir, cedar, oak, maple, alder—when you fly over, you wouldn't know that there's a different, less inviting landscape down underneath. Below this Garden of Eden there's a natural hell. Not many people ever see it, but it's there. It's an underworld honeycombed with thousands, maybe millions, of tunnels and vents and caves. You don't want to go there. If you do, you want to be careful. Bone-breaking careful. That underworld is deep enough and twisty enough—and plain old spooky enough—to make getting lost as easy as slipping on an icy sidewalk. Like that sidewalk, things can look fine when you start out, then suddenly, WHAM! Your world goes upside down. A lot of people have never come back from Darkhorse. It's an aspect of Eden that the tourist bureaus tend to de-emphasize in their pleas for out-of-staters to bring their money and Come Visit!

Anyway, Dan and I were about fifteen when we stumbled onto something under Darkhorse—something that at first was fun, but bit by bit started to scare the skin off us.

Now please understand something. Whenever Dan and I went into the caves, we knew enough Boy Scout and camping lore to blaze our explorations. Maybe not in the conventional way, but we did it. We were careful both in Darkhorse's tunnels and in the ones near Salem. Darkhorse was by far the more complex system, though, so that's where it was most critical. Blazing was a simple process. We got cans of orange and green fluorescent spray paint from the autobody shop that Dan's older brother ran over in Albany. Using the paint to blaze the rock walls of the tunnels and vents was easy enough. Every few yards, we'd spray on a backwards arrow. It was orange at Dan's caves and green at mine. That way, if we got into trouble and needed to get out fast, we could follow the trail of arrows without having to think. That's important, because when panic wiggles up your backside, thinking gets a lot tougher.

These days, they've got hand-held, inertial guidance positioning computers. They're supposed to be amazingly accurate. Nothing against 'em, I guess. But it's hard to go wrong with a blaze mark. Not impossible, but hard. Unlike computer directions, blazes don't disappear if the battery runs out or a software bug starts getting hungry at the wrong quantum moment.

Despite our best efforts at preparation, I think we were incredibly lucky to have survived. That bothers me a little, because I don't know where luck fits into the reason equation. I *do* remember how rambunctious and eager we were to explore the caves. Especially Dan. Given our state of mind, there's no way we could have sprayed enough arrows, or done a half-dozen other things, to be as safe as we ought to have been. On the other hand, our ignorance probably helped us come on it down there. The thing. The thing that never should have been there, not by any science we were taught, not by anything we could grasp at the time. Our ignorance enticed us to look into a side passage that perhaps we otherwise would have missed. If we hadn't dipped into that passage, I wouldn't be telling you any of this.

As it was, we went deeper into Darkhorse, and ourselves, than we ever could have dreamt. So, no, although I don't remember how we originally found the entrance to the caves, I clearly recall how we discovered that bizarre tunnel. It was the one with the voice that howled in perpetual pain.

Chapter 2

We were on a roll that summer vacation. Regular junior spelunkers. Nowadays they'd call us cavers. I hear some of the cavers use the term "worms," but I don't like that one. If the other cavers had gone through what we did, I doubt they'd go for it, either.

We'd just finished a few days of poking around at the caves near Dan's place. They had proven to be dreadfully disappointing; just a few straight passages and a lot of dead ends. Too simple to be interesting. Or so we thought at the time. "Boringsville," as Dan had put it. We shrugged it off and decided to tackle Darkhorse instead. Action was the name of life for us then. We hoped that Darkhorse would provide more of a challenge, a few dares, and perhaps some stories we could brag up at school. That's what I wanted, anyway. Dan usually had more exalted, scientific interests.

Mind you, while we were amateurs we weren't running a Tom Sawyer operation with candles and hope. Dan's family wasn't rich, but was certainly well off. So he'd purchased miners' lights and hard-hats, nylon ropes with grapples and mountain tackle gear, including pitons for the steep passages and drop-offs, good back packs, first-aid kits, and so on. The point is, as young and eager as we were, neither of us was stupid. Inexperienced, sure. But not a pair of dummies. When the chips are down, I think most kids are smarter than adults typically anticipate. When we went down into those caves, we had every intention of making it back out with all our body parts intact. Bragging rights bruises, sure. But nothing more.

We hadn't considered that it might also be necessary to take precautions to protect our minds.

Okay, where was I going with all this? Oh, yeah. Let's pick it up down in Darkhorse. A few things are starting to come back to me. I remember now *that* the caves existed was an open secret. More of a legend, really. Darkhorse had evolved into the grist for threats from parents who couldn't get their kids to quiet down at night. I recollect how my own mother told me that the Darkhorse Demon would get me if I didn't go to sleep. We didn't have the boogie man in our house, but believe me, the Darkhorse Demon served well enough in our young imaginations. As we got older, we transformed the Darkhorse Demon into stories of ghosts of lost prospectors and crazed, escaped killers, rapists, and molesters. Because of their nasty reputation, not many people ventured into the caves—not thirty years ago, not now. Childhood legends had a way of sticking with you when you grew up. Just to make sure, the city had put up a sign outside the caves, urging extreme caution and telling people that they were on their own as far as liability was concerned.

As you might guess, that sign was a neon invitation to Dan and me. We'd both read Ayn Rand's *Atlas Shrugged* the previous summer and we were suddenly men of intransigent reason. We didn't buy the legends about demons, gods, ghosts, or poltergeists—at least not consciously—and delighted in any opportunity to debunk them. In high school, we had a minor reputation for annoying everyone from UFO fanatics to young Christian missionaries. As far as we were concerned, it was all in the same box labled "superstition." Hence, to go into the caves was to strike a blow for the ideals of the rational mind—of which we were, of course, the self-appointed vanguard. True, the idea of defying the authorities' fuddy-duddy conservatism added a certain dash of spice to the adventure, but we'd convinced ourselves it was for a nobler purpose.

The caves' entrance was small, maybe four feet square. It was largely overgrown. Even the sign was mostly buried in the brush. Ah, okay! Here comes another memory shard: we'd never have known about the cave entrance but for Dan's older brother Sam. He was a great guy, but also a blooming alcoholic. The advantage of his condition was that after consuming his third or fourth beer in a row, it was possible to get Sam to tell us almost anything. One hot, slow July afternoon out back of his shop, he mentioned that he'd been down in Darkhorse when he was a kid. He made up some nonsense about hearing screams and moans down there and running out with his ass barely intact. *That* served to whet our appetites. We kept at him until he laughingly, but somewhat nervously, told us how to find the entrance. Despite the booze, his directions had proven remarkably accurate.

We'd taken the first day to blaze what we called the ground floor. That was a level of the caves with a few, short dead-end passages. It wasn't much. Not a single demon. No dead bodies of crazed crooks or unlucky prospectors. So we headed down to the second level. We called that one the basement. You needed rope to get there.

The connecting passages, two of them, were sheer drops. The first opened directly above an underground stream that gushed from beneath a rock face and then disappeared into a gurgling drainhole a few yards farther on. We took turns lowering each other down, but it was a bust. There were no side vents from this tunnel and nowhere to go. Worse, the water smelled overpoweringly like fresh pig manure. Dan said the stream probably drained through from a hog farm up higher on the west face of the butte. It wasn't the kind of water you'd want to lug around in a canteen. The first passage down to the basement was clearly a no go.

Taking the other drop down was a quick, 20-foot rappel. The next two days we spent in that part of the basement. It was more like what we'd been hoping for. There were dozens of unexpected turns and smaller passages, branching and breaking off in intriguing ways. There was a huge room large enough to play tennis in. I recall how utterly awed we were, gazing at that cavernous space. Dan said it would've been a good place to be during a nuclear war because of the rock above and around us. He said it would be easy to seal it off from the outside. Looking back, I kind of doubt that. I think there were way too many passages to make it practical.

At one end of the room there was a cold, clear spring. It bubbled up from the rock and ran along the side of the room. It eventually emptied with a roar into a wide, deep passage that angled sharply down. We never did find out where the other, manure-smelling stream ended up, but it had missed this part of the basement.

At first, we thought that was it, the sum total of the Darkhorse system. Teenagers are easily bored and we were getting antsy. However, Dan insisted that because the spring emptied down, there must, naturally, be even lower levels. He said we just had to keep looking.

"Dan," I asked, "don't you think maybe that springwater is falling into the *only* way down? Maybe that's all there is below here—just an underground stream tunnel."

In the yellow glow of my miner's light, I could see Dan shake his head, a slight frown on his wide brow.

"No, ol' bud, I don't think so," he replied in that prematurely deep voice he had. "That's not exactly how these cave systems work."

I took his word for it. This is a good place to mention that Dan was what you and I would call a super-genius. He had an IQ that soared out over 200 and an almost infallible memory to boot. A year earlier, he'd done us both a favor by auditing some classes on West Coast geology at Oregon State University in Corvallis. He was always taking ©18classes over there. The professors loved him. Any one would have rolled out a four-inch thick red carpet for Dan on the hope than when he finished high school he'd come and be a star pupil.

Standing there in the dim light, I looked at Dan and knew his giant brain was probably thinking of five times as many things as mine. Sure enough, in a couple seconds he said, "Come on!" and trudged off towards the low end of the room.

We went past the drainhole and Dan aimed his light along

one wall as he walked, touching the surface now and then with his fingers, looking for something. I didn't know what, so I asked.

"Clues," he said.

Great. For all his mental firepower, Dan was sometimes not a chatty guy. Although, when you got him a bit tipped with alcohol, it could be like Hoover Dam opening its floodgates. That made it difficult for Dan to get any action because the only time he'd get tipped was when he got sexy and then the poor guy would talk the ears off a girl instead of figuring out other, more basic things. If Dan was any example, I think high IQs are like veins of ore; they run pretty rich in some places and awfully-poor in others.

Dan had stopped about twenty feet ahead of me when I saw his headlamp suddenly disappear. I heard a muffled, "Jackpot!" I hurried forward as he stepped back into view from around a little hidden bend in the wall.

"Find another way down?" I asked, feeling like an idiot as soon as I'd said it. What else would he have found?

Dan always took my normal mental speed in good cheer, though. I was grateful for it. I knew he could have left me choking in the head-dust, but he never did.

"You got it, ol' bud. But it looks like it's going to be ropes and pitons all the way."

"How far is down?" I asked doubtfully. For some reason, there was a tiny red warning light blinking at the very back of my brain.

He brushed my question off with, "Ah, who knows?"

I presumed that was supposed to make everything all the more fun. But then, seeing the worried look on my face, he slapped my shoulder and laughed.

"Hey! Just kidding!" he said. "It looks like about a forty-foot drop to another floor. No problem. You ready?"

"Well, uh, what about the time, Dan?

"Forget the time. This is *opportunity!*"

I tried to force a grin of agreement. After all, we did have food and sleeping bags and we would surely find enough spring water. Even if the water turned bad, we had chlorine tablets to sterilize it. I guessed that we could stay down another week if we really had to, although it wouldn't necessarily be a stroll on the street. That's what reason told us, and we were Rational Men, weren't we?

"Okay, just a second," I said, pulling out a can of green spray paint. I marked the entrance to the next level with a backwards-pointing arrow.

"Good man," Dan complimented me. It was a casual remark, but it made me feel like a million bucks. He was my age, but I always felt younger, like an admiring little brother. No matter what their actual ages, I think super-smart people seem much older than the rest of us. Not in all ways, no. But in more ways than you can count on both hands.

We drove a piton into a thin crack in the dark gray volcanic rock just above the drop-off, secured the rope, and rappelled down, Dan first. The floor sloped about twenty degrees at the bottom. We found ourselves standing in a small, angled chamber. There were a half-dozen vents and tunnels leading out of it. Two of the vents were too small to get through, even if we wriggled on our stomachs. Spraying arrows as we went, we started exploring the other four openings. We went systematically, moving clockwise.

The first passage had no side branches. It wound on for a good quarter-mile back and up into the heart of Darkhorse Butte, dead-ending in a pile of rock rubble. Dan chipped some of material with a miniature prospector's pick. He looked at it in his palm, turning it this way and that, muttering, "Hmmm" several times. Finally he declared that the rock probably was part of a series of cave-ins from when the original volcanic cone began to seriously erode as it turned itself into an ordinary butte. He said that the tunnel we were in was undoubtedly once a major gas vent. How he knew that I hadn't the foggiest notion. I wasn't even sure what a gas vent was. Dan was funny sometimes. When I asked how he knew something, some days he'd be a fountain of information. But on other days, he'd shrug one shoulder and keep quiet with his eyes blank.

Maybe it sounds silly, but I think he was self-conscious about how much he knew. I think he held it in sometimes so that people wouldn't believe he was lording it over them. Over the years, I'd figured out that he was self-conscious about his extraordinary brain power. Sometimes I'd feel sorry for him, almost scared for him. I wanted to tell him that he didn't have to feel embarrassed around me, his first cousin and best buddy. But I guess I hadn't quite developed the guts or the method for that kind of intimacy. Anyway, Dan wouldn't have liked it. Maybe kids today can say those things. We couldn't back then. We grew up with too many tough guy ideas. It was the early 1980s and in rural America that often meant that it might as well have been the 1950s.

The next passage was a score. It wasn't long, but after a few hairpins, it leveled off into a room about twenty feet wide. Running down the left side was a series of small pools. Always, a foot or so higher, a smooth rock floor ran along the right side. You could stroll by and look down into pool after pool, running into one another through tiny waterfalls. It was beautiful and kind of surreal, almost artificial. But the beauty wasn't what got Dan's mind going. What excited him was that in some of the pools there were fish—pure, white, weird fish without any eyes. I'd never heard of anything like it, but Dan had read something in *National Geographic* or *Science* or one of those many magazines and journals that his folks got him in order to keep his hyperactive brain from eating itself up with too much boredom.

After several tries, he managed to make a net out of his T-shirt and catch and dissect one of the squiggly little devils. He said they were carp, kind of like wild goldfish. He said they had gotten trapped down in Darkhorse way back when, maybe millennia ago before the Indians were around in Western Oregon. I guess mutations can take some wild turns. Dan naturally knew all about them, and used more than a couple quick sentences to explain everything to me.

After we got back to the room where the rope dangled from the level above, we debated whether to pull it down. We decided not to. We had plenty of rope, and it was, after all, our main way back upstairs. If we took it down, we'd have to scale the tunnel to return to ground level. That seemed like a lot of pointless trouble, especially if we needed to get out fast. That little warning in the back of my head was blinking a bit brighter, but for the life of me I couldn't have told you why. It was an odd feeling, kind of like the ache that sometimes flashes at you a couple days before you get the flu. It felt like something was *coming*, but I didn't know what. At the time, I thought that maybe those blind fish had given me the creeps. I couldn't identify a reason for the sensation, I tried to mentally brush it off. I certainly didn't tell Dan about it. Rational men handle their misgivings, right?

According to our watches, it had gotten pretty late. We were feeling the strain. Our legs and backs throbbed from unusual use and we had innumerable scratches and scrapes that we didn't remember getting. You have to take spelunking fairly slow. It's not like hiking out in the woods. There you know that if you get lost the chances are good that you'll find your way out or someone'll spot you eventually. In a cave like Darkhorse, with its maze of tunnels and passages, especially if no one's terribly familiar with it, it's not like that. You have to depend on yourself for everything. Dan had told me that the first rule of spelunking was to assume that no on would find you. That way, you'd be more likely to never get lost in the first place. He said it was an economic principle that applied to all human action; it was called a "negative incentive."

"Is that like saying if we're not careful, we'll get our asses fried?" I asked.

He laughed and said, "Yeah, I'd say that's a fair summary of the principle. But it wouldn't look good in an Econ 101 textbook, though."

We rolled out our inflatable air mattresses that Dan's folks had bought us the previous summer, blew 'em up, and laid out our sleeping bags. I put on an extra sweatshirt I'd brought. Down this far, the caves felt chillier and damper. It was as though by descending, we'd somehow moved out of summer

and into fall. The sensation contributed to my growing uneasi-
ness. It felt as though—well, as though something was *off* and
getting worse. It was almost like someone had begun to trail
us, silent and purposeful and not necessarily friendly. I'd been
glancing over my shoulder for two hours, but Dan hadn't
seemed to notice. He'd been too busy chipping rocks and ana-
lyzing anything he found. I considered sharing my feelings with
Dan, but decided that tough guys didn't do that. Besides, my
logic circuitry couldn't find anything substantive to focus on. I
told myself that the whole reaction was probably a stupid hor-
mone-driven emotional impulse.

Chapter 3

I growled to myself and stuffed the messy, bothersome feelings into a dusty corner in the back of my mind.

We had some jerky and dried apples for dinner while we talked about what we'd seen so far. There wasn't anything around to build a fire with, but we'd brought a small kerosene lamp. The place was passably cheery. At least it was for Dan. He apparently wasn't uneasy about anything. I'd seldom seen him so excited. He showed me bits of rock and pebbles and pieces of sticks and seeds and other plantlife that had washed down from above, discoursing merrily about their implications. This was one big science adventure for him. I envied him his ability to keep his rational faculty in the forefront. Mine seemed doomed to constant struggle. At the same time, it made me look up to Dan even more than I always had. Maybe he wasn't John Galt, the ideal man, but I figured he was a lot farther along toward being enlightened than I was. After awhile, his assured manner lifted my mood. I was tired, but feeling relatively okay again.

We decided that if either of the remaining two passages was likely to lead us down farther, maybe to a sub-subbasement, it would be the next one in the rotation. When we aimed our headlamps down, we could see a steady slope for almost fifty yards. It looked like it would be an easy trek.

Our talk drifted to movies and girls and we were both grinning and chuckling when all of a sudden Dan's smile disappeared. He held up his hand for me to be quiet.

"What?" I asked.

"Thought I heard something."

I perked my ears for a minute, but I didn't hear anything. I started to smile. Dan kidded around sometimes. I found out in our forensics class that he could act, too. Practical jokes were part of his personality.

I started to say, "Gotcha, Dan! The giant no-eyed goldfish are gonna grab—"

Then I heard it, too.

It sounded like a far-off animal. It was howling, like a creature badly frightened or hurt. The sound was coming from the next passage, the easy one that we were supposed to head into in the morning.

I shivered involuntarily. I looked skeptically at the lamp's flame. Moments ago it had been cheery. Now it seemed like a puny hedge against the dark unknown.

"Geez, Dan," I began, "what do you suppose—"

He cut me off with a nonchalant wave of his hand. He was grinning broadly, even though we could hear the howling louder than ever.

"Nothing to worry about, ol' bud. Didn't mean to raise your hair. It's just that I'd never heard one before."

"What?" I demanded peevishly, ankle deep in adrenaline. "Heard *what*?"

He calmly opened his canteen and replied, "Air currents." He took a long swallow of water, wiped his mouth, and added, "You know, the flute effect."

"The what effect?"

I asked it a bit raggedly as the howling carried on like a trapped bloodhound. I wanted to trust that Dan would come up with his usual explanation and make me feel safer. I wanted it badly.

Maybe he sensed it, because he gave me an appraising look and said, "In passages like some of these, you've always got air currents. Some of 'em get pretty strong. When they blow across openings, such as small vents, they can make goofy sounds like that."

He pointed, unconcerned, at the guilty tunnel.

"Well . . . I guess, if you're *sure.*"

"Hey," he said, softening his voice as he all but openly acknowledged my fright, "I know what it is. I've read about this effect. Believe me, this is what they described. Nothing much to worry about."

I nodded, willing myself to accept his explanation, trying to drive away the banshees in my brain. The fear gradually, reluctantly trickled away, like oil running off my skin. Dan, after all, knew so much. He had to know what he was talking about. He always did, right? I looked at his big, wide, intelligent face. I couldn't see any reason to doubt a face like that. He was smiling and relaxed, and simultaneously concerned for me, his same-age, somewhat younger brother of spirit. We were cousins, but I always thought of him more as an older brother. I think he knew it, too, but never mentioned it. He accepted the relationship as natural, and so did I.

Soon we were joking around again, even though off and on we'd hear the howling in the background. Sometimes it would fade away, then come back stronger, but it seemed progressively more distant now that I wasn't scared of it. Finally, Dan said he was beat, yawned, stretched, and rolled over. Before I could have said five sentences, he was snoring.

It was too abrupt. I resented him, always did, because of how he could shut off the world and drift into the safety of sleep. I never could do it that fast or that easily.

Almost as soon as he zonked out, the howling started to get to me again. Was it maybe a little closer than before? Or was it purely my nasty imagination? No matter how I forced myself to remember Dan's scientific assurances, the eerie sound ate at me. The fright started to slither back, like a big snake advancing half-seen through the brush. I hugged myself, shaking slightly, and looked longingly at Dan's broad back. I thought how I'd like to snuggle up for comfort—and immediately felt awash in horror and guilt, thinking that maybe I'd developed hidden perverted tendencies. That's how we looked at it in those days, in rural Oregon. Any thought of that kind of physical contact with a man, no matter how innocent — well, you just weren't supposed to go there.

After sitting hugging my knees to my chest for about twenty minutes, my eyes finally started to feel sleepy. I made myself curl up in a ball inside my sleeping bag and I tried to imitate Dan's courage and lack of worry. I guess it worked, because before I knew it, Dan was shaking me awake and telling me that breakfast was on.

I sniffed. Something smelled wonderful. I squinted. He'd rigged up a little cooker using the kerosene lamp. He was frying two small fish.

"This boy's been workin'!" he said briskly, catching my eye and winking.

I sat up in my sleeping bag and rubbed my eyes with my knuckles, tasting the overnight paste in my mouth.

I stretched and asked, "Where'd you get the fish?"

He lifted one eyebrow and squinted conspiratorially with the other eye. Then I knew where he'd gotten the fish. He'd gone all the way back to the pools, leaving me alone to face the howling. At first, I felt a flash of anger. Then the sensation evaporated because his leaving was proof that he trusted his own judgment as to what the howling was. Dan would never do something like that if he wasn't convinced that I was safe. He purely wouldn't. He'd defended me against bullies and had saved my life at least once when I'd almost fallen out of a tree. That's the kind of guy he was — smart *and* committed to doing the right thing.

I cocked my head, listening for the howling. It wasn't there.

"How long's our noisy vent been asleep?" I asked as casually as I could, getting out of the sleeping bag and working on some stiffness in a shoulder.

"Hmmmmm," he replied. "Hadn't paid much attention after I figured out what it was."

"I noticed. You dropped off like a refrigerator over a cliff last night."

He smirked and said, "Always do."

"Hey, Dan," I asked after I rolled up my sleeping bag and

fixed it to my pack, "how come the sound just stopped cold like that?"

"Happens. Wind, you know. Not constant anywhere, not even on the surface. Although—"

He was frowning slightly.

"Although what?" I asked, almost absently. My mind was more on the frying fish than on last night's events. Food is a big attention getter when you're a teenager. It can overcome a lot of odds to march front and center.

"It's just that I thought cave breezes tended to be more stable," he said.

"Why would that be?" I inquired, getting out our old tin Scout dishes that we always took along. I edged closer to the fish, which Dan was turning over and salting as he talked.

"Temperature differentials. A lot of air flows through caves like these, ol' bud. All the time. But they tend to be pretty cool when there's spring water running through. Acts like a natural refrigerator and the ground above acts like insulation."

He flopped a sizzling fish into my tin.

"Anyhoo," he continued, "you've heard that cool air is heavier than warm, right?"

"Yeah, I guess."

"Take my word for it. The cool air is always flowing out through any lower openings of the caves. That draws warmer air in through the upper vents, like the one we came in."

An idea struck me. I asked, "But wouldn't that turn around in the winter, I mean, when it's colder outside?"

"Could. If it's cold enough. Then the warmer cave air, insulated from any quick outside temperature change, would rise out the upper tunnels and draw cooler air in through the lower ones."

I tried a bite of fish. It wasn't bad. Bony, but kind of like underdone halibut.

I pointed my fork at Dan and said, "Sounds like you really don't think the howling should have entirely stopped."

"Uh, no. Must be some natural fluctuation of which I'm unaware. Funny how these things work sometimes."

His frown deepened and I caught him looking sideways at the vent.

"Uh-huh," I replied, "real funny."

He suddenly didn't sound convincing to me. I felt myself growing angry again about his leaving me to go fishing. I didn't say anything. In a complicated way, the situation made me feel closer to him. I'd never fully realized that Dan didn't know everything. Oh, I mean, sure, I knew it intellectually. But I hadn't felt that way. It's hard to react otherwise when ever since you've known him, your best friend has been a walking library. Then I got irritated at myself as it hit me just how much I'd let myself depend on Dan over the years. Something tightened up inside me, like a clamp closing a pipe. Out of nowhere — or so it seemed — I decided to start doing more of my own thinking. The resolution made me feel good, and at the same time a little disloyal. I shook it off and grinned wryly to myself. I had a long way to go before I became the ideal man of reason. *Boy* did I have a long way to go.

We ate our fish in silence, neither of us with much gusto. I caught myself trying to keep myself facing the howling vent, which was supposed to be howling, but wasn't. I looked at a forkful of fish. When I thought about them having no eyes, I felt nauseous. I felt like I'd somehow compromised myself to the howling, or whatever was making it. It was a nutty thing to feel, and I knew it. Even so, I couldn't shake it for several minutes and almost had to throw up twice. I think Dan noticed, but he kept his peace and let me work it out.

We both dawdled, trying to delay going into the howler tunnel. Neither of us was willing to admit it then, but I think if either had suggested that we forget heading down to the sub-subbasement and just high tail it out of there, we would have done so in a second. At least I would have. Dan, maybe; maybe not. Twice I caught him looking sideways at the vent. What that gaze meant, I couldn't say for sure. Part suspicion, maybe, but also determination, like when you rise to a challenge, the "you're not beating *me*" look that guys tend to get. Yeah, and a third part of his expression was the intense curiosity that Dan always got when faced with a puzzle.

Since neither of us was going to admit anything that a rational man "shouldn't" be feeling, we fought it by loading up our gear, taking deep breaths, and heading down. I sprayed a lot more arrow-blazes than I needed to.

Chapter 4

The vent descended at a fairly steep, straight angle for a couple hundred yards. The character of the rock began to change, too, looking less gray and black and more creamy and light brown, sometimes slightly greenish. There were small stalactites here and there, too. We hadn't seen any of those before in Darkhorse. The passage suddenly branched off into a warren of tunnels, tiny rooms, and squiggly vents. It was considerably different than the levels above and the perspective was all screwed up. If it hadn't have been for gravity keeping our feet in one direction, I wouldn't have been able to tell which way was up. There was also an odd smell in the air, almost like burnt electrical wiring. It came and went for awhile, then finally faded away. Dan frowned some more, but offered no illuminating explanations.

We hiked for a long time. The system went on and on, like a dozen giant rock-burrowing worms had taken years to eat out hundreds of interlacing, twisting tunnels, bending back on themselves, heading up and suddenly sideways, then down, forward, and sideways again. Periodically, it would open up into huge, smooth-walled caverns. Dan blabbed on about ancient magma bubbles and geologic upthrust intersections. His curiosity was again at fever pitch, but I was hard pressed to keep up with him, either physically or mentally. He could be Mr. Science Observer, but I had to remember to keep blazing our way with the green fluorescent paint. It was about all I could handle. I didn't have time to participate in a strolling seminar. I was getting worried, too. In some places the paint wasn't sticking well. The walls were getting too damp and had begun to glow with their own, competing luminescence. Dan said the glow probably came from an odd type of light-emitting bacteria or fungus.

When I realized that I'd been subconsciously trying to save paint by spreading out the arrows, I yelled at Dan to stop.

"What?" he said over his shoulder, hardly paying attention, moving on without me.

"Hold up a minute, Dan!"

"Yeah, ol' bud," he said impatiently, "in just a minute. First, I gotta see up there what that—"

"Dammit, Dan!" I shouted. "I said *stop!*"

He spun around to glare at me. I had never used that tone of voice with him. I'm not sure anyone had—except maybe his older brother, Sam, who had never been particularly intimidated by Dan's brain power.

Dan glared at me for a moment, then said, "Jeez, *okay,*" with a barely blunted hot edge, almost like someone my own mental age for a change. "What's the problem, bud?"

"Dan, listen," I said carefully, holding up a can of paint and shaking it. We could hear the hollow rattle of the ball. "I'm almost out of this stuff. I didn't bring enough. Besides, it isn't working anymore."

"Huh, what do you mean it's not working? Of course it's working. Paint is paint."

"No it isn't. Would you *listen?* It's the walls, Dan. They're getting too wet for the paint to stick well. Half the time I can barely see what I've sprayed."

"Your point being," he said.

I swore in exasperation. All of a sudden I felt like I was talking to a stubborn third-grader.

"The *point,* Dan, is that it's getting too dangerous. We vowed to blaze our trail carefully. Now it's impossible. We could get lost without even trying. We've got to go back."

"Back? *Back?*" Dan muttered, as though it were a foreign word. "But I haven't seen all—"

I took a deep breath and interrupted sternly, "No buts, Dan. We'll starve in here if we can't mark our way out and get lost. It's time to turn around — now."

For a second or two, I honestly didn't know if he would do it. He was looking longingly in the other direction. I'm sure his scientific gray matter was letting him see and enjoy a lot more information than I was able to process. To me, everything in Darkhorse was becoming damp, highly unattractive, and confusing — except for the certainty that we had to get out. And, of course, that stupid red light in the back of my head was blinking overtime.

"Well, " he said, "okay. Okay, I guess you're right. But we've gotta come back down here again soon, okay? There's all kinds of stuff I need to examine and categorize and it would be a shame to not explore the — "

I cut him off with an frustrated wave of the hand. I didn't bother to answer him verbally. I let my actions say it. I started hiking back.

After a few seconds, he fell in alongside. Within five minutes his curiosity and spirits were back on top. When adventure was afoot, it was hard to keep Dan down for long. After awhile, we decided to take a break for some crackers and cheese and a little water. Dan asked me one of his out-of-the-blue, got-nothing-to-do-with-anything questions, for which he was notorious.

"Hey, ol' bud," he said, "you ever been over to the other side of this butte?"

"Huh, what do you mean? To the base? Of course not. It's off limits. Everybody knows that."

A few years earlier, the US Army had unexpectedly bought up several thousand acres of the rolling terrain that constituted the back slopes and steep switchbacks of Darkhorse. Paid top dollar and in one case even used eminent domain under some national security act or other. Then, in no more than six months, the Army surrounded everything with a fourteen-foot electrified, razor-wired fence. Signs every fifty feet carried heavy duty warnings about the nasty things that might happen to unwary trespassers.

For awhile, a lot of truck convoys and massive cargo heli-copters moved in and out, carrying who-knew-what. Clearly, the Army was putting together something important. What it was, no one could say. The city fathers didn't particularly care—or pretended that they didn't, considering that the Army didn't tell them anything. The city was more interested in the big business expected from a new base near a small town. It never materialized. The Army didn't allow anyone on the base to mingle with civilians in Lebanon. Not ever. There was no "base boom."

Eventually, the Army traffic settled down to only two or three chopper flights a night, sometimes none for several days. The Army took pains to avoid flying over populated areas. All we could see from Lebanon was an occasional bright light right before the choppers landed behind the butte. The machines were quiet. Almost soundless. They seemed to come and go toward the south-southeast. Dan said that was the general di-rection of the big US air bases and secret test ranges in Califor-nia and Nevada. He thought they might somehow be connected with the Darkhorse base, though he never revealed the rea-soning behind that conclusion. If he had any. Sometimes Dan did more speculating than true theorizing. Not often, but some-times his imagination ran away with him.

"Well, I've been there," Dan said. "That is, I found a way to see into that base."

I looked at him blankly in the dim light.

"What the hell are you talking about?" I asked, my skepti-cism clear.

"I found a spot where you can climb a fir tree and get a pretty good view of the facility."

"Uh, isn't that impossible? It's all supposed to be hidden. A lot of people have tried."

"Not from this one spot."

I cocked my head. He had that serious look in his eye. Ap-parently this *wasn't* speculation or a practical joke build-up.

"Okay, so what did you see?" I asked.

He took a moment to choose his words. In the low light, for just a second, the shadows played tricks on his face. They made Dan look much, much older. I shivered. It was as though, for a fleeting moment, a window opened up into his adulthood — and he didn't look happy. Not at all.

"So what did you see in the base?" I repeated, trying to shake the eerie sensation; it was making my back feel like spiders were running around under my shirt.

"Well, to be honest," he said, disappointment crossing his face, "not as much as I'd hoped. Mainly a bunch of plain, government-stamp buildings. I watched off and on for two days and a night. Saw one humongous copter come in with something slung under its gut, though."

"But get this," he said, leaning closer. "A bunch of guys in *hazard* suits unloaded it. That makes me wonder if we've got some sort of chemical or biological weapons factory up there. Might even be connected with radiation weapons research. Something, that's for sure."

"Jeez," I exclaimed. "What's going on?"

He shrugged and leaned back, his face becoming darker with shadow.

"Don't really know," he said. "Too much speculation. Insufficient data. But here's something else to make you think. When I went back again on the third day, the tree I'd climbed wasn't there."

"Huh?"

"Gone," he said, his face growing grim. "Like it had never existed. Like it had never grown there at all."

"They knew you were there," I said.

Dan nodded sagely. "Of course. Must have spotted me with infrared or other sensors. Motion detectors, maybe."

"But how'd they make a full-grown fir tree disappear, Dan? That's impossible, isn't it?"

"Got me. There was no sign of equipment, of chainsaws, footprints, nothing. Figure this: where the tree had been, there was just this big ol' boulder that looked like it had been there since God made the world."

"Oh, *man!*"

Dan grinned at my reaction.

"So what now, Dan?"

"Huh? Waddya mean?"

"I've got to see this place! You've got to take me there!"

"No way," he said, shaking his head. "That tree was the only vantage point around. Believe me, I checked it out. Used some surveyor equipment from OSU to verify it. The only angle from which to see into that base and catch sight of the buildings and helicopter port was from the tree. It's gone now. The Army saw to it and there's no point going back just to look at a big rock. Let's not beg for more trouble. We've got enough to handle right here."

He stood and stretched and said, "Well, let's march."

End of subject. I felt frustrated and cut off. Why did he tell me that story if he wasn't willing to share any of the experience by at least showing me where he'd been? Usually, Dan was eager to show off something like that. I shook my head. Well, Dan had an offbeat side to his personality.

We hadn't gone far — progress was necessarily slow in those winding worm passages, with me forced to verify the blaze marks every few yards to make sure we hadn't made a wrong turn into some likely looking side tunnel — when the howling started up again.

We stopped and stared at each other. I could feel the hair raise on my forearms. I knew why, too. The howling was coming at us from *above*. Somehow, despite our trailblazing, we'd gotten turned around and the howler, whatever it was, was between us and the way out.

Chapter 5

C rap," I said flatly.

To my shock, Dan didn't react that way at all.

"Great!" he said with a whoop and a playful slap at me.

"Great?" I asked, astonished.

"Oh, yeah, man! This means we'll be able to find the vent that makes that sound. I thought we'd have to put it off for another time. Now I'll get to see it up close!"

"We'll see it all right," I mumbled under my breath, "or whatever *lives* in there."

He heard the comment and snorted.

"Aw, come off it, ol' bud! You're not buying some sort of supernatural crap, are you? Nothing lives down here. There's nothing for it to eat!"

I snapped back, "Well, we ate fish. Fish live down here, Dan. Why not something bigger?"

"Oh, hell," he said. It's clearly a matter of available food supply. Anything big enough to be dangerous would need more to eat than a few little fish."

His attitude was getting short and more than a touch condescending. I didn't like it. My temper went off like firecracker in a mailbox.

"Sure, anything you say, brain-boy!" I shouted. "But you haven't truly explained why the howling stopped and started. And I think you were scared yourself when you realized you didn't understand it. And things *can* live down here and maybe you're wrong about how big they can get! So fine, it's irrational in your book to feel that way, but I'm not going to pretend I don't. I'm glad you're not scared, if you really aren't, but I *am*, and at least I know I am, so . . . so, well, don't talk to me like I'm some kind of idiot, okay?"

I turned my face away for a minute, feeling flushed, trying to cool down. I noticed that my fists were clenched against my legs, which were trembling from anger. After a moment, I felt Dan tap my shoulder briefly. I looked at him in the yellow glow of my miner's light and saw that he was smiling a little. I could tell it wasn't easy.

"Look. Uh, well, see ol' bud, it just that . . . I'm sorry. I can't always— Aw, darn it. I didn't mean to say that you're an idiot. I don't hang out with 'em!"

I wasn't completely cooled off, but his last remark made me feel better. I held out my hand. He grinned broadly and took it.

"All I gotta say," Dan intoned gravely, shaking his fist menacingly at the direction of the howling up ahead, "is that if there is something making that sound, it better be ready for a couple of mighty tough dudes!"

The bravado was catching. We punched each other on the arms, puffed up our teenage chests, and strode forward again.

The feeling didn't last.

It was getting harder to find the paint marks I'd made on the way in. The walls had been wetter than I'd thought. In some places the paint had run down in barely perceptible fluorescent rivulets. We had to take turns going ahead, one of us keeping the other guy's light in view, in order to find the next undeteriorated mark while not losing the last one. This worked for awhile, but there came a point where I couldn't stay in view of Dan's light and hadn't found another blaze mark. Not even a smudge that *could* have been one. I walked back to Dan and grimly shook my head.

"No go," I informed him. "Can't locate another blaze. You go up and try. Maybe I'm not seeing straight."

I hoped I was right about that, but Dan tried and couldn't find a blaze, either.

"If we could get beyond this wet area somehow," he noted, "the marks might be easy to spot again."

"Right," I said. "And if I could just jump eight feet, I'd hold the world's record. The question is, how do we find the dry area without getting even more lost?"

"We don't leave footprints in here," Dan noted, scuffing at the rock floor. "Next time, I guess we'd better devise some kind of back-up system for the spray paint."

"Uh-huh," I said sarcastically, "next time."

Then Dan dropped a nice big one on me.

"Uh, ol' bud, I have to tell you something. I've been doing some mental arithmetic, and I don't think these miners' lights will last much longer."

"Wonderful," I said, feeling more cynical and defeatist by the moment. "That means *we* won't last long, Dan. We're goners if we don't have light."

We decided to sit and think about it while we had a snack. We got our butts cold and wet and our feet ached. We lit the kerosene lantern—which itself would be out of fuel in a few days even if we only used it an hour or so twice a day—and turned off our miners' lights to save their batteries. Meanwhile, the howling, moaned and undulated in the distance. We listlessly chewed some dried meat and crunched a little peanut brittle. After a few minutes, the food made us feel slightly better, but not much.

"How come it's so damn wet in here?" I asked. "I mean, why is the moisture covering all the walls this way?"

"I've been trying to figure that out, too. Best I can come up with is that maybe Darkhorse isn't quite the dead volcano that everybody thinks it is."

"You've got to be kidding."

"The only thing I can think of that would produce all this moisture is steam."

"Steam?" I waved my hand around. "There's no steam here. Not that I can detect."

"We're seeing the condensation effect. We're not close enough to the source yet to see actual steam. I figure it's from volcanic heat deep underground. Kind of like those vents on Mount Hood and Mount Baker that the geologists are always keeping their eyes on."

"Guess I hadn't heard of that."

"I've mentioned it," Dan said. "You've just forgotten."

"Yeah. I seem to forget a lot."

"Hey!" Dan blurted, snapping his fingers. "I think I just had an idea!"

I chuckled and said, "You're *always* having 'em."

"Listen," he plowed on, "if we can find a place where we can actually see some steam and not just infer its presence from wet walls, we might be able to find a way out!"

"I'm more lost than ever, Dan."

"Don't you see? Listen," he explained, edging closer and looking me in the eye, willing me to understand, "where there's steam, there's water. Water has to flow down from somewhere to hit the warm rocks that make the steam. There's no guarantee, but if we followed the water source back up—"

"But hell," I responded, getting the idea, "it's sure better than sitting on our asses and going blind!"

We rushed to put our gear away and got ready to start moving once more.

"Uh, just one tiny problem," Dan said, unconsciously shifting slowly from foot to foot.

"Let me guess," I chimed in. "We can't see any steam now, so how do we know where to head?"

"Right."

"Wait a minute," I said. "Wouldn't the walls be wetter closer to the steam?"

"Might be," Dan said, rubbing his chin, "might just be. You could've just pulled our behinds out of a sling."

The unexpected compliment knocked my mood up three notches. Dan didn't send praise my way too often. He didn't mean anything by it. He was always too busy with the "out there" world.

We started a hunt for wetter walls. It was easier said than done. Logically—that is, by teenage logic, even though we thought we were being highly adult—we had it all figured out. It was like looking for the blaze marks. One of us would stay put and the other would go from vent to vent, checking for higher levels of condensation on the rock. If he got out of sight, the other guy would yell for him to come back. It wasn't a bad system as far as it went. It just didn't go far enough. Problem was, all the walls felt damp and it was impossible to tell for sure if one was damper than another. Eventually, Dan hit on an idea that worked.

We'd brought some newsprint notepaper with us and we tore it up into little strips. Timing the seconds on our watches, we touched the end of a strip to a wall and marked with a pencil how far the moisture climbed, wick-like in five seconds. The farther it climbed, the wetter we figured the wall had to be. Dan made us take multiple tests on each wall, explaining that the law of averages worked better for us that way. Presently, we settled on a couple of tunnels that we thought were definitely carrying more moisture. We couldn't tell the difference between them, though. Not a problem. Out of one—leading upward—was coming the howling sound.

Our emotional impulse was to go down the other, quieter one. Of course we knew we couldn't. First, we'd obviously passed the howler somehow coming down here—maybe by taking a by-pass passage when the howler was in one of its quiet phases. Maybe in there we'd find some of our original blazes. Second, if a breeze was making that sound via the flute effect, then, it being summer, we might be able to follow the draft backwards, up the warmer air source. That source, Dan assured me, had to reach the outside one way or another. Third, if there was water flowing into the howler, it had to come from somewhere and maybe we could follow it up and out.

We couldn't think of anything better, so we started in. Meantime, we'd come up with a way to prevent ourselves from getting permanently lost, or at least anymore lost than we already were. We lifted the idea from the old fairy tale of Hansel and Gretel. Instead of using bread crumbs, we dropped little bits of the notebook paper behind us to mark our passage. I gulped and hoped we wouldn't run out before we found more intact blaze marks. Despite the breezes that would whip through the caves unpredictably, the paper shreds stuck fast to the wet floor.

We hadn't been hiking for more than five or six minutes, when Dan yelled, "Shine your headlight up there and tell me what you see."

I stepped up beside him and aimed my light where he pointed, up the tunnel. The air was definitely hazy there. It should have made me feel better, but didn't. It was too much like looking at a dark, foggy street in some old creep show episode. My brain, by its own odd willpower, brought up Rod Serling's pressed velvet voice saying, "Imagine, if you will, two young adventurers, in over their heads and striding up a one-way passage into the *Twilight Zone*."

I forced the thought aside and instead tried to imagine that I was John Galt, ideal man, thinking things through, lucidly, calmly. It helped more than I expected.

"Is it . . . *steam*?" I asked, unsure of what I was seeing.

Dan laughed and slapped my shoulder, "Yeah, that's my guess. Keep dropping those paper bits, Hansel. Just to be safe!"

"Guess that makes you Gretel," I said, slapping him back.

He chuckled, doing a mock curtsey. "Let's go see what the Wicked Witch has got for us."

What we got was thicker, eerier steam — and a louder howling echoing through the caves.

My mood was on a rollercoaster. It nose-dived again within minutes, but Dan's did the opposite. Right then, if I could have packaged his mood, I could have sold it as anti-gravity.

After about ten minutes, the tunnel warmed up. The steam grew as heavy as airport-closing fog. The howling was so loud at times that it was nearly deafening. It kept rising and subsiding to its own measure of time. Dan rattled on about possible causes, inventing hypotheses like other people invent gossip. I relaxed a little. One thing for sure. No animal could scream that loud. I felt myself blush, realizing how much I'd feared that the howler really might be some kind of demonic tunnel monster. In some of us, childhood legends die hard, whether or not we've consciously decided to be Rational Men. I also realized that I was hearing a kind of wet, hissing noise mixed in with the howling. Dan nodded his head like everything made perfect sense to him. Maybe it did, but it unaccountably irritated me. In another thirty yards, I understood.

The tunnel had widened into a small cavern about as big as a two-car garage. Several stalactites hung from the roof, with accompanying, squat stalagmites beneath. Dan said parts of the system here had to be limestone.

"Limestone?" I asked. "But I thought this was all volcanic stuff down here."

"No, you've forgotten. I mentioned it earlier when I was telling you about fold formations. The two types of geology are not mutually exclusive," he explained. "Sometimes volcanoes erupt through old seabeds, which have sections of limestone created from pressure."

"Oh."

The passage continued through the cavern. We could see where it exited on the other side. In the cavern, off to one side, through clouds of steam, we spotted a gurgling pool.

Dan said, "Aha!"

The water in the pool was draining down a hole at the bottom. In a minute, the pool was completely empty. Dan quickly made us steppp out of the cavern. We waited warily. In a couple minutes, the hole started to howl and hiss. Boiling water and steam geysered into the room. In a few seconds, all activity stopped. The pool was draining again.

"Well," I confessed, giving Dan a sideways grin, "that's my monster."

Chapter 6

"Okay, now what?" I asked, remembering that we were still lost. After all, we'd never been in this room and there were no blaze marks visible.

Dan rubbed the stubble on his jaw. I momentarily envied the fact that he *had* stubble. I didn't have much more than an anemic patch of peach fuzz on my chin. Minor things sometimes loom big when you're fifteen.

"Hmmmm," he said, helpfully.

"I guess we oughta continue on through, right?"

"Yeah, it seems like we head up after we cross through the steam room. Up is the direction we want."

"Looks to me like the fog's thicker out the other side, too, Dan. Lot more of it than on the way in, wouldn't you say?"

"Well, it would be," he said, thrusting his lower lip out in a show of certainty, "at least for a ways. Doesn't seem to be much of a breeze coming through here, though. Thought there'd be a steady current up and out."

"Why isn't there?"

"Not sure. Maybe the steam keeps this part of the cave warm enough to reverse the air flow locally, you know, like a high pressure weather system."

Sounded thin to me, but I bit my tongue and didn't say anything. With me dropping more of my paper crumbs, we moved on. Dan took the lead since he knew better than me what to look for; or at least he said he did.

Just beyond the steam room, not more than sixty or seventy feet, he stopped suddenly and said, "Whoa! What is this?"

He was looking right and left, then above and below where he was standing.

I hurried up beside him. I whistled. A perfect, oval ring of what looked like shiny stainless steel wrapped around the tunnel. The ring was about six inches wide and protruded roughly an inch from the rock facing. Its existence flabbergasted me.

"Guess we weren't the first ones to find this particular passage," I observed.

Dan shook his head. He was running his fingers over the surface carefully.

"Man-made, for sure. Good engineering, too. But I don't understand why it's here. What's it for? What does it do?"

"Maybe it's part of a mining shaft," I offered lamely.

"Never heard of a mining operation around here. Besides, this is way too high-tech for a mine. They wouldn't use finished metal like this for simple shoring. This is more like something—oh, like you'd see in a laboratory or an industrial fabrication facility."

We examined the ring more closely. From some angles, it was slightly iridescent. It threw my depth perception off. When I tried to touch it once, I jammed my finger because my eyes told me it was a couple inches away.

"It's like I can't always see it right," I said to Dan.

"Yeah," he replied, running his palms carefully along the edge over his head.

I imitated him and did the same along the ring's bottom.

"Hey, look down here!"

I was on the ground peering at the edge of the metal, from the direction in which we'd come. Right where the ring passed seamlessly into the rock, we could see what looked like writing stamped into the surface of the steel, or whatever it was.

Dan squinted and moved his lips.

"What does it say?" I asked.

"Symbols of some kind," he answered, squeezing his face closer, cocking his head. "No, not symbols. I'll be darned—it's Cyrillic!"

"Sir-whatik?"

"Cyrillic. It's an alphabet. Our words are written in Arabic letters, but some places in the world use these instead."

The little red warning light was blinking like a strobe as I asked, "Like *what* places, Dan?"

Dan looked up at me from his bent position and said slowly, "Like some Eastern European countries, and—"

"And? And? And *what*?"

"Russia."

Our eyes locked in silence as insects of nervousness scampered along our skin.

I didn't know how to respond. It was too wild to work in my computer. I stood up instead and did a masterful job of looking perfectly retarded while Dan the genius started to yak irrelevantly about the history of the Cyrillic alphabet and how some saint of the Slavs started it up.

"Dan," I interrupted his monologue.

"Yeah?" he said, standing and brushing his pants.

"What does this mean, this ring being here like this?"

"Haven't a clue. But I suspect that whoever built it contracted the job to the Russians."

"The Russians are our enemies," I pointed out. It was true, of course, back then. All this happened as the Cold War was going full bore. Almost nothing came into the United States from Russia then. They were the bad guys. They were the murdering jerks who were going to cook us and our families with nukes and then piss on our ashes.

"Can you read Cyrillic?" I asked.

Dan shook his head. "I have been intending to get around to it, though."

He meant it, too. He said it like you or I would say we meant to see a movie. When we'd been in French class together, I remembered how easily he'd learned that language. It was like he absorbed it by breathing. He never seemed to study. He remembered everything, as far as I could determine. He could instantly pronounce things right, too. If he decided to learn Russian, I was sure that he'd do it as fast and flawlessly as he'd learned French.

We decided to give the ring one more going-over for good measure. However, we found nothing new except that the ring felt slightly cool to the touch; that is, cooler than the cave walls that were coated in condensation from the steam. Curiously, nothing seemed to condense on the ring. Dan thought this was "maxo-weirdo," because cool metal should have been a most attractive condenser. As he put it, it would act like a cold can of beer on a humid summer day. There was no moisture on the ring; not a drop; not even a hint of a wet sheen. Dan said it was as though the ring was operating by his own laws of physics. He said it jokingly, but I thought there was a shade of seriousness to the remark. Or maybe it was just my emotional mind fighting with my rational mind. Why couldn't the two ever get in step?

After a few minutes, we figured we'd seen all we could. We hoisted our packs and trudged on silently, keeping to what appeared to be the main passage, each lost in his own thoughts but trying to watch for blaze marks. I'm sure Dan was probably doing equations or higher geometry in his head or something sophisticated. All I was doing was churning with confusion, fear, and anger at myself for being the way I was, getting myself into so much trouble, and at a loss as to how to get out. I consoled myself with the thought that Dan the Genius was in the same boat and that, after all, we were only teenagers.

We saw nothing else like the ring, but it turned out to be far from the weirdest experience we were to encounter. There were stranger events ahead. Without a smidgen of a clue, we were walking straight into them.

"One thing I don't get, Dan," I said after a couple minutes, breaking the brooding silence that had hung over us.

Dan looked at me and cracked a pained smile, "What's that, ol' bud?"

"Why was that geyser back there so irregular? Aren't geysers supposed to go off like clockwork, you know, like Old Faithful over at Yellowstone?"

"Most of 'em do, but sometimes not. I read about it. Depends on the source of the water that pours into the hot places. If you've got an irregular source, then I suppose you'll get an irregular geyser. They're on record. It's not as unusual as it probably seems."

"Maybe it depends on how often the pigs piss above us on the butte."

"Yeah," he said, laughing too sharply, "yeah, I guess maybe it does."

"You know," he continued after a pause to retie a shoelace, "there was something else about it. I took a pretty good look down that geyser hole as we passed. It was lined with polished steel."

I stopped and stared at him.

"Huh?"

"What I mean is that the howler was positively no natural phenomenon."

I stood with my mouth hanging open. I couldn't think of anything to say. Dan shrugged, offering no elaboration. It was too bizarre to register on my reason meter. Either I needed a better meter, or I needed to avoid this kind of adventure. I shook my head, sighed, hitched my pack into a better position, and started walking again.

The tunnel climbed at a gradually steepening angle. The steam was so thick that I could hardly see Dan, even though he was only a few feet ahead of me. We'd been trudging along for several minutes when he stopped and I almost ran smack into him.

"Hey, what's up?" I asked as he turned to face me.

"Notice anything funny?"

"If you mean that this stuff's disorienting as hell, yeah, I feel like I can barely keep my balance."

"Hmmmmm," he said, scratching his nose with a thumb knuckle. "Must be the fog. Throws off our visual perception. They say sight is closely tied in with balance."

"Whatever, it makes me kind of dizzy." I brushed my hands over my eyes like you do when you run into a cobweb string in the woods.

"Same here," he said, "except I've never actually felt dizzy in fog."

"Makes me feel almost—" I broke off, embarrassed to say what I was thinking.

"Like what?"

"Don't laugh," I said.

"I won't."

"It's like gravity isn't working right."

"Uh-huh. Well, it's theoretically possible, you know."

He launched into a diatribe about gravity vortexes that some scientists thought might make water run uphill and screw up airplane compasses.

"I thought that was a bunch of optical illusion show-biz," I protested.

"Not everyone thinks so," he responded. "Lots of twisted stuff in the real world. Maybe maxo-weird answers to it, too. When we can find 'em. I'm not sure it's always possible. I don't think man is advanced enough to find all the answers—even when he really needs 'em."

I didn't particularly like the answer.

After a short spurt of hiking, things started to look better. The air cleared and the disorientation passed. We squatted our lanky frames down on opposite sides of the tunnel and broke out a little food and water. I munched some jerky and he gnawed on a piece of hard chocolate. We didn't say much and didn't take long. We were both eager to keep going. I think Dan was finally looking forward to getting out of those godforsaken caves. We were both wet and grimy and bruised. I wanted a hot shower and a good meal and a long sleep.

In no more than ten minutes, we were at it again, making considerably better time now that we didn't have to act like two-thirds of the three blind mice.

Dan had stretched his lead out quite a bit, but was in easy sight of my miner's light. This rising tunnel had few branches. Those we saw were mostly small, and all headed back down. Down was not an option anymore.

I looked up and noticed that Dan's light wasn't moving. I

yelled with forced cheerfulness, "Find a stop sign?"

He didn't respond and his light stayed stationary.

"Hey!" I jibed, "they outlawed sleeping on your feet!"

There was still no reply. As I drew closer I could see that Dan was standing sideways, looking at something in or on the wall of the tunnel. At first I wondered if he'd found another ring. His body angle looked odd to me, like when a camera catches someone stop-action and off balance.

I hurried up to him and said, "What's the big idea not answering when your buddy calls?"

Chapter 7

Not possible," he muttered.

I leaned closer, trying to catch his eye.

"Huh? What's eating you," I asked, waving my hand in front of his face. He looked dazed.

"That," he said, raising a finger and pointing at the wall. "Not possible."

I looked. I'd never actually felt goosebumps rise on my flesh. I did then. On the cave wall, pointing ahead, was an orange fluorescent arrow. It was the kind of arrow I sprayed, all right. But it was the color that we'd agreed to use in the *Salem* caves, forty miles away.

"Not possible," Dan mumbled several times in succession.

I didn't like the way he kept saying it. I didn't like Dan acting like that about anything. Dan was my reality anchor.

I took a deep breath and tried to clear my brain of the vines of fear that had been pushing in.

"Look, Dan," I said, trying to put conviction into my words, "it's a coincidence. That's all. Somebody else had the same idea we did and has been in this part of Darkhorse before. It's just another entrance that we didn't know about. Anyway, orange paint is as common as fence posts. No big deal."

When he didn't react, I stepped in front of him, grabbed his shoulders and shook him, speaking slowly, like to a little kid, "C'mon, buddy! Let's shift that big brain out of neutral!"

That brought him around.

He shook his head and smiled sheepishly.

"Yeah, yeah," he said. "Dunno what I was thinking. That steam and disorientation must have gotten to me back there."

"Could be," I said, nodding sympathetically. "Look, let's pull it together and get out of this joint. Somebody's painted us directions and we'd be stupid not to follow them."

"Right, sure," he said. He glanced back at the arrow. "It's just that it looks so *much* like the blaze marks you make."

"Hey, I know two girls at school who have handwriting you can't tell apart. Coincidence, Dan. Happens."

But inside, as I looked at the blaze again, I got the same feeling. The blaze *did* resemble my style, complete with a little squiggle on the tail of the arrow. And there was the fact that Dan had a photographic memory.

I had to suppress that line of thought. I couldn't let the vines of fear start crawling into my head again. I needed to keep my logical mind in gear and get us out of there. I grabbed Dan and began walking in the direction that the arrow pointed.

"Dan, I don't care what your fabulous memory says, it doesn't make sense. I'm not gonna let you give me the slitherin' jeebies anymore. You're the one that's supposed to stay on the road of reason, right? Well, now is the time! Don't go all emotion-wobbly on me, buddy!"

Dan shuddered and seemed to pull out of it. "You're right. What the hell have I been doing, anyway? Sorry. Let's go soak some sun."

He seemed to have snapped back to reality, but I remained wary. To my chagrin, I found that I didn't quite trust Dan like I always had. Under building pressure, I'd seen him *lose* it. No, not big-time. But enough to cause doubts. Well, Ideal Man is supposed to be independent, too, right? That's what I asked myself, adding under my breath, "So where's your independent thinking been all these years, ol' bud?"

I don't know if Dan heard me or not. If he did, he didn't show it.

We found more orange arrows as we went. I kept telling myself that just because they looked so darned familiar, just because my mind and arm could *feel* myself making the motions that would create those kinds of blazes, it was no excuse to toss logic through the sewer grating.

Dan, who had seemed okay for awhile, started to worry me again. He kept frowning and saying things in a low voice under his breath about how his memory had never let him down before.

"Knock it off, Dan," I said sharply, throwing him a look that meant business.

He looked down guiltily and slogged on.

Even though we were convinced that we were on our way out of the caves, our legs were feeling incredibly heavy, like when you have to walk too far in soaking wet jeans. I knew that it was more than simple fatigue. Underneath what was left of our bravado we were as scared as little kids in their first thunderstorm. Not just me. Dan, too. He handled it differently. Well, I rationalized, it *was* our first experience of the kind. Maybe being frightened wasn't so bad. Maybe it was nature's way of making us wake up. I wasn't entirely clear on what I meant by that. I shrugged inside.

Maybe, I thought, doing our best in a situation is all we ever have as human beings. Not the ideal. Not perfection. Just the best we can muster in a particular circumstance.

I shook my head and smiled ruefully. I was getting entirely too deep for myself.

I kept us marching along, my jaw clamped tight in determination. It wasn't long—although it seemed longer then— before the passageway took a slow left turn and we saw light streaming down a straight stretch that wasn't more than a couple hundred yards long. When we saw it, we both glanced at each other and abruptly halted. This was exactly how we remembered things going out of the entrance of the caves near Salem, 40 miles away.

In one sense, you'd have thought we'd break into sprints at that streak of daylight. But we didn't. We were reluctant to move at all—either forward or back, like raccoons trapped in the middle of a road, unsure about which way to turn to safety.

Dan again started muttering, "Not possible."

I let out a few choice cusswords that I seldom used, grabbed his arm, and forced him to walk with me up to the entrance and into the sunlight.

It must have been about ten in the morning. The sunshine would have felt good, except that off in the distance it was illuminating Dan's folks' farmyard.

"Listen," Dan said to me as we strode through the tall grass and scrub toward the house, "I don't know what happened to us in there. I know I lost it for awhile and I'm sorry. But I have this overpowering feeling that we shouldn't talk about it to my folks yet. I don't know why, but I think we should try to figure it out on our own before we let anyone in on what we went through. How about you?"

"Yeah, no problem," I said. I'd been thinking nearly the same thing.

"Do you think we *can* figure it out?" I asked, getting an inexplicably lonely feeling.

Dan inhaled deeply, held his breath for a moment, then blew it out in a long, controlled sigh.

"Everything's got to have a reason," he said with conviction, "everything. Sooner or later we ought to be able to understand it."

"It's the 'later' that I'm worried about," I said.

"You and me both," he said, his face haggard.

We met Dan's mom in the kitchen. Aunt Edna loved Dan to no end and, I'm sure, loved me, too. However, there was a puzzled streak to her smile.

"Why, what on earth are you two doing back so soon?" she asked, punctuating the question with a spatula she'd been using to stir cake batter.

"Uh, so soon?" I asked. I don't think she even noticed the question. Aunt Edna had a tendency to override conversations with her own thoughts.

"Did you forget something?" she asked. "Or— Oh, my!"

She noticed our grimy clothes for the first time.

"You two look terrible! If I didn't know better, I'd say you'd been gone for days!"

"Well, of *course* we—" Dan started to say in his my-mom's-always-a-tad-whacky tone, but I elbowed him in the ribs. He was about to spill stuff we'd agreed not to mention. Besides, there was some kind of undercurrent running through the room and it was making me uneasy. The little red light in my head was blinking furiously. I wanted to get us away from Dan's mom *fast*.

"It probably looks that way, Aunt Edna," I said in my best forensics persuasion voice, "but then how long do you think two teenagers *ought* to take to look like this?"

She laughed, "Oh, you're probably right. I've said before that teenage boys are the only creatures other than two-year-olds who can get filthy as sin before they have their shirts on in the morning. Even so, I would have thought you'd be grown up enough to keep from getting disheveled for at least an hour."

Dan's mouth fell open and I took over again before something stupid spilled out of his royal genius.

"Uh, we have to get some things we forgot up in Dan's room, Aunt Edna. Sorry, but we're in kind of a hurry."

She winked and chuckled and waved us off with her baking spatula.

I hustled Dan out of the kitchen and we pounded up the stairs to his room.

When I closed the door and had some assured privacy, Dan immediately burst out, "What was Mom talking about, 'at least an hour'?"

I shook my head and held up both hands.

"Dan, what color is your mom's hair?"

"Huh? What's that got to do with anything?"

"Answer the question, Dan. What color?"

"Well, it's always been kind of a strawberry blond."

"I thought you told me she has this 'natural' thing about not using hair dyes."

"Sure, so what?"

"When did she change her philosophy? Just now downstairs I distinctly saw red hair on her head. Not strawberry blond—red, red as a carrot."

"Aw, that's nuts," Dan said. "She'd never dye her—"

Then he stopped because that amazing memory of his was seeing red, too.

"But I just can't imagine her doing that," he said, scratching behind one ear.

"Me neither. And since when did she like checkered gingham curtains on her kitchen windows?"

"Since never. She hates that stuff. Says it looks like old bread wrappers."

"Right. And since when would she be so forgetful that she'd think her son and nephew had been gone an hour when in fact they'd been gone for days?"

"She wouldn't. She's whacky, but not that whacky. Besides, she's the one I inherited *my* recall genes from."

I nodded and said, "Now you're starting to get it. Look around, Dan. Look at the stuff in your room. Look closely."

He did, then whistled in astonishment.

Superficially everything was normal. But little things were off. Dan was a big fan of Sean Connery's James Bond movies. He didn't like the Roger Moore versions of recent years. He always had an old *Goldfinger* poster over his dresser, a gift from his older brother Sam. It wasn't there. In its place was a picture of Moore. Dan thought Moore was a wimp. Dan had always been a houseplant nut. He loved to grow them in his windows, experimenting with different soils and nutrients and so on. In place of the plants on the sills were clay sculptures; some quite new, showing a lot of talent. But Dan hadn't had an interest in sculpture since the fifth grade. The bedspread was a light blue. Dan preferred dark blues and blacks. His 35-gallon aquarium was there, but it didn't have Dan's Japanese Koi that he'd raised for two years from the fry stage. Instead, somebody'd turned the aquarium into a terrarium with a couple of ugly lizards inside. Dan had once had a short-lived fascination with reptiles, but that had been years ago. The list went on, right down to the missing chemistry set that Dan had owned since he was seven.

"Omigod," Dan said softly. His lips and face looked as

drawn and white as mine felt. His eyes turned to me as he said in a tight, anguished voice, "Ol' bud, this isn't my home!"

"I don't think so, Dan," I said.

"Let's get out of here," he said urgently.

We bolted out of "his" room, down the stairs, and through the kitchen so fast that we couldn't make out what Dan's "mom" yelled, looking bewildered and beautiful in the red hair that she'd never had.

Chapter 8

A few minutes later, we stood just inside the cave entrance with our hands braced on our knees, huffing and puffing. We'd still had our packs on when we'd run from the farmhouse up to the caves.

"We've got to go back," Dan said, panting.

"That is *not* your place," I said emphatically, thinking that his brain had gotten derailed again.

"No, I don't mean that. I mean that we've got to go back down through the caves. All the way."

"Aw, Dan, that's as crazy as a three-dollar bill."

"No, wait! I've been thinking. Somewhere inside there we had to have taken a wrong turn."

"That's the understatement of the week."

He shook his head. "I'm not saying this right. Listen, I think I know where it happened."

"Oh."

I was interested. A theoretical wrong turn was one thing. A wrong turn that we could pinpoint was another.

"I think it had to be in that section where we both got our balance out of kilter," he said, his eyes starting to gleam. "I believe it was back after we passed the ring. I've been recalling some obscure physics papers I stumbled on down in the basement at Oregon State one rainy afternoon last year when I had time on my hands. Some researchers think there might be such a thing as alternate realities. Has to do with quantum possibilities. They think that all things that could happen, *do* happen, somewhere. Or at least a lot of the stronger possibilities do. They believe that we might be able to control passage among them, so — "

"So they're nuts, Dan! That sounds like low-grade fantasy or science-fiction."

"Well, I used to think so, but . . . " He waved his hand around, indicating the cave walls. "But maybe not now. I can't come up with any other hypothesis. Can you?"

He looked at me for a second like he thought I could. No way. That kind of reasoning was Dan's department, no matter how screwed up on simpler things he could get sometimes.

I sighed, looked down into the gloomy cave passage, glanced at Dan, smiled weakly, lifted my face, and said, "Okay, what choice do we have? Whatever happened, whatever we stumbled into, this place sure isn't where we belong. Let's go."

Dan held out his hand and we shook.

Low on supplies and tired, we headed back down into the caves, determined but grim.

We had surprisingly little trouble finding the steamy area and the geyser. We also found good green blaze marks. As we'd theorized, they were in a passage that branched off from, paralleled, and by-passed the geyser area, reconnecting later on. In a few hours we walked wearily out the entrance to the Darkhorse side of the caves.

We didn't get back to my house, though. Oh, at first it looked like mine. As with our experience at the farmhouse, there were those little differences. Things that didn't belong. Parents who didn't look and act quite the same.

That's why, after resupplying ourselves and stealing some rest in the woods, we went back through a third time, trying to slip into the reality that was ours. It didn't work. So we tried again. And again. And again. Over and over.

Sometimes everything was so close to what we remembered as "real" that we almost stayed. But we never did. We knew we had to find exactly our reality, because it wouldn't do to have two of me and two of Dan in the same place. Several times early on we accidentally caught glimpses of our other selves, and it spooked us to our cores. It was like that old saying about someone walking on your grave—except that this felt like someone was walking on your life. I'd never felt anything like it, and I never wanted to again. After that, we were careful to avoid any chance of contact.

We took odd jobs to stay alive, always careful to get work away from our home towns so we wouldn't be recognized. As best we could, we continued our education. This mainly consisted of Dan loading up on books and teaching himself, and tutoring me on the side. Basic knowledge of things like physics and biology seemed to be the same everywhere, in all the alternate realities. Oh, there were some differences in history, such as who invented what, but nothing substantive. Dan took heart from that. He said it meant that there was an overarching super-reality in which all basic laws applied. Whenever we could, we went back through the caves, trying to locate our original home reality.

Quite a number of times, Dan brought in jury-rigged electronic devices and test equipment that he'd "borrowed" from various locations. I remember a Geiger counter and a miniature mass spectrometer and a few other things. Most of it was beyond my grasp. Dan did his genius-level best to analyze the ring and anything else he could in order to figure out, and maybe control, what was going on down in the caves. He never succeeded.

Then, on one of our trips through, we made a major mistake. I guess it was bound to happen some day. Dan went through that disorienting section just a little too far ahead of me. When I went through, he wasn't there. No poof. No fizzle of electrons or snap of a reality gate. Just gone. He'd edged into somewhere else a tiny bit different. It was enough. I haven't seen him since. Not in almost thirty years.

Oh, yeah, sure, I've looked for him. Desperately. After all, he was not only my cousin and best friend, but my only link to my old life. After awhile, though, I got tired of the search. It was as simple as that. Alternate reality or not, I had to make something of my life. I'd reached my early twenties and it was time to get on with it. I couldn't keep searching forever. Dan was lost at sea. You can't wait on life's shore forever.

My life in this place—I call it Reality 1000, because that's the number I decided to stop looking at—isn't that bad. It's close to what I grew up with. There's only one crucial difference. In this place, by sheer good fortune, a person like me never existed. When I came into town, I was just another immigrant. I'd been planning to leave the state when I reached Reality 1000 in order to avoid running into anyone who'd recognize me from my old life—or mistake me for my counterpart. It was nice not to have to do that. It was nice to have the familiarity, however askew it was in smaller ways, to cushion the building of a new life.

I've had to learn some things, of course. Like how to use a twenty-four letter alphabet. No "y" or "z" in this one; and to remember to shake with my left hand; and to play cards with an extra face (a Prince, ranked between the Jack and the Queen). Nothing major.

As with the laws of physics, there seemed to be a law that prevented any major deviation from the norm in cultures. Most of the time, anyway. I stepped into some frighteningly nutty places now and then.

There was one where the United States had degenerated into a theocracy that used cannibalistic rituals to celebrate holidays. There was another where most of the people looked like how the Neanderthals were described in anthropology journals, complete with heavy brows and hunched walks, and yet everything else was almost identical to my old world. There was one place that turned my blood into icewater. There were ruins of human civilization, but no humans. What flora and fauna existed did not appear to resemble anything earthlike. What had happened there, I never found out. I was too scared to stay and explore. But it made me realize something Dan and I had never thought about: if we could slip through that reality gate, what *else* might slip through? What legends of gremlins and sprites and so on might be explained by "normal" creatures sliding from their own place into an unfamiliar one? Well, I had enough trouble. I tried to keep thoughts like that from crowding to the forefront of my mind.

And now? Oh, I'm fairly happy here. I'm all right, I guess. Despite the ancient ache that grinds inside my skull occasionally, missing Dan, missing the old world and all that was and might have been, I continue to hope. I particularly hope that I'll see Dan again. Because, you see, if he didn't slip into a really bizarre place, a primitive one, perhaps, where people are so different that they lynched him or stoned him, thinking he was a freak, or witch, or madman, then there's a chance. There's a chance that that curious, magnificent mind of his will find an answer to what happened. It might find a way to control the slippage from one reality to another. Then, he ought to see the arrows I sprayed in Darkhorse, pointing the way into this world, the last blazes I ever made, the ones with the words, "This way ol' bud" sprayed above them.

I hope that's enough for him. It's all I could think of, and I'm sure he'd understand. You have to trust a guy like that, right? I mean, if you can't, what good is *any* reality? What good is reason? And I still believe in reason. I do. There's an answer to all this. There must be. Dan would say so.

Oh, one more thing. That mysterious ring down in the caves? It was always there. Always the same. Did it have something to do with the reality-twisting—if that's what it was? I thought it was probably caused by that disorienting passage later on, but maybe not. I keep thinking about it, and if I do, I'm sure Dan must. And if he does, then he'll figure it out. I have to trust in that thought.

There's more to the story, of course—like how it ties into World War 3—but I can hear them coming for me. I'll have to tell you the rest later. I will, too. This was only the first part of what I was able to get recorded. I know I can't keep the rest inside much longer. No man should have to. So I'll stop here and regroup. Wish me courage. Reason will prevail, won't it? We have to hold onto that, right?

Part Two:

THE REVELATION

Chapter 9

At first, the message looked like a joke. It came late on a Friday night. Well, it was early Saturday morning, but late enough for the Friday night carousers to be in bed or under the table. Too early for the local birds to be chortling and cawing for the sun.

I'd just checked my watch. It was almost two. I'd folded another terrible hand of poker. A lousy pair of fours. Aces and a possible straight showing against me. It had been a bad night.

It wasn't so much that I was down fifty bucks. That was normal. I've always been a mediocre card player. No, it was a bad night because I needed the sleep, but felt compelled to stay awake as long as I could. Going home meant drifting off in front of the TV on my creaky old couch in my small apartment. Oh, my place wasn't the problem. I'd grown fond of that little dive on 12th Street. It was quiet, cheap, and in good condition. The problem was that sleep meant nightmares. They were nightmares of a type I thought I'd junked long ago, way back in my early 20s. Amazing how we can fool ourselves. I probably should have known better. But then, I guess I'm known for *not* knowing better.

The bad dreams had been coming for a month, ramming into my subconscious like a flurry of fat fists. Lost in the caves again. That's what the nightmares were about. Losing my cousin Dan again. Trying to find him. Over and over. Always failing. It had really happened, of course. Not quite thirty years ago. Now my stupid subconscious had decided to rerun it night after night. Win or lose, I'd play poker as long as anyone wanted to deal the cards. Nightmare Cinema was not exactly my favorite movie house.

I'd just put some creamer and a half teaspoon of sugar into my sixth cup of coffee when I heard the doorbell ring.

"Get that, would you, Joe?" Frank said from the table, nodding at me. "Probably the pizza."

An all-night pizza joint had recently set up in town. Fred, our 300-pound never-say-no-to-food player, made full use of the delivery service during the poker games.

"Yeah, okay," I said.

It was Frank's house, located near the end of Rose Street in the small town of Lebanon, Oregon. It's where we always played poker on Friday nights.

I went down the hall toward the front of the house, rubbing my eyes and yawning. I opened the door. A light, warm breeze wafted in from the east. It was August and Oregon was doing its annual impression of a Southern California spring. The moon was out, etching everything in dark, sharp shadows. I could smell honeysuckle blossoms. I looked down the walk and off to both sides. There was no one there. No pizza box, either. Thinking that some kid had rung the bell for kicks, I shrugged and started to close the door. That's when I noticed the envelope on the welcome mat. I picked it up. It was plain and white, the kind you could buy anywhere.

It had my name on it.

"What the heck?" I said, glancing up and down the walk again. Nothing.

I tore open the envelope and squinted to read the note in the moonlight. It was a brief message, written in hastily printed block letters. They looked vaguely familiar.

The note said, "Meet me at the ring in Darkhorse this morning at six."

It was signed, "Dan."

Blood pounded in my temples. My legs got weak. I had to lean against the door frame and make myself breathe.

There was only one person this note could be from. Trouble

was, he'd been gone, probably dead, for almost three decades. Or so I'd thought.

Cousin Dan also had been my best friend. When we were in our mid-teens, we'd lost track of each other down in the caves under Darkhorse Butte east of town. I got out of them, but Dan didn't. After all these years, I recalled it as clearly as if it had been the night before.

We'd edged through a kind of perpetually foggy section of the tunnels. Dan was walking a little ahead of me, just out of sight, probably no more than ten yards. When I reached the place where he should have been, he'd disappeared. There had been no place for him to go. In that section of Darkhorse, there were no side passages, no places to hide, no nook to duck out of sight for a practical joke. It was as though he'd stepped into another reality, through some kind of space-time twist, like what you see in cheap science-fiction movies.

I don't profess to understand it. I think it's beyond my mental firepower. Mind you, I'm not stupid, but I'm no genius, either. Not by a long shot. Not like Dan. His IQ was so high that if you caught a ride on it, you'd find yourself in orbit. It was practically unmeasurable. Don't get me wrong. I'm sure there *was* a reason for what happened to us — somewhere. However, it was beyond me. It was for smarter people. Sure, Dan said everything had a reason and at least in theory I believed it. You might say I religiously held onto the idea. Faith in reason, I called it these days. It worked better for me to think of it that way; more wiggle room. Dan would have cringed, though. As a true Objectivist, a follower of Ayn Rand's philosophy, he'd have called it a contradiction in terms. Or maybe just stupid. He always said you had to *trust* in reason, not have faith in it, because reason derived its value from evidence and proof, not from mere belief.

Well, whatever. I guess I'd become slightly cynical over the years. I mean, how could you fully trust reason after you'd experienced something like I had, where no matter how hard you ramped up your old rational circuitry, no meaningful answers were forthcoming? How could you engage your rational faculty when the facts squirmed away like slimy eels whenever you tried to make sense of them? Sometimes it got so eerie and unreal that I didn't feel fully *me*. Sometimes I felt like— well, like there was a part of me that was locked away, cut off from the rest, and if I could just get at it I could figure everything out. I suppose that doesn't make much sense, either. But that's how it felt. That's one of my problems, too. My feelings too often shoulder aside my rationality. Sometimes I feel like there's a constant war going on inside my head—and I don't have much control over either camp.

Standing there in the darkened doorway of Frank's place, I tried to will myself to shed the bad memories and self-doubts. I looked at the note again, turning it this way and that. I briefly wondered if it was a joke that one of the guys at the poker table was playing. Naw, couldn't be. No way. I'd told none of them about Dan or the caves. They hadn't known him. In fact, none of them knew much about my past. I wanted it that way. I'd worked hard to keep the old days vague. I'd even adopted a false name: Joe Smith. Original, huh? Actually, it was perfect. Undistinguished, like me. I'd gone to a lot of trouble for a full set of fake ID from a black market house down in the Los Angeles area.

I folded and pocketed the note and closed the door. My heart was going twice normal speed. I wouldn't need any more coffee to stay awake now. The adrenaline would keep me going. I looked at my watch. Under four hours to go. If I were to meet Dan—or whoever this was—down in Darkhorse by six, I figured I'd better get my rear in gear.

Pleading fatigue and enduring friendly catcalls of "Shorttimer!" and the like, I cashed out of the game and headed home. I knew they'd probably continue playing until eight or nine, maybe 'til noon. These guys were poker addicts. Hell, if the Darkhorse meeting was a bust, maybe I'd rejoin the game.

From the back of my bedroom closet, I pulled out my old miner's cap. The battery was dead, so I took a moment to replace it with a spare. I dragged out a dusty rope and a set of pitons. I worked fast. I stuffed my Leatherman tool in one front pocket and a small flashlight in the other. I put some jerky in my shirt pocket and filled my old canteen with fresh water. On impulse, I strapped on the shoulder holster for my Smith & Wesson Centennial .357. It was a late 90s model, before Uncle Sam forced the makers to produce so-called smart guns — the ones that IDed you with print and grip sensors, took forever to fire, and hence were useless in a fast-moving situation. Dumb guns, I called 'em. I checked the cylinder. I usually used .38s in it and it was full. I pocketed a handful of extra shells. Then I shrugged into a light coat, and locked up. There was no one to leave a note for. I currently had no love life. I had no relatives to wonder about me. My friends knew I was a loner. They didn't care. I often disappeared for a week or more, working out of town or going on long camping and other pleasure trips.

Not quite two hours after leaving Frank's, I was at the butte. The sun was reddening the sky behind Darkhorse. A dormant volcano, the butte reminded me of a drab old buffalo hunkered down against the dawn. It looked unsettling, almost threatening. I parked my beat-up GMC pickup in the brush off a spur of an abandoned logging road. I figured that I could leave my rig there for weeks and no one would find it.

Chapter 10

It took me only a few minutes to locate the entrance to the caves. "Aw, hell!" I mumbled, resting my fists on my hips and glaring at the problem.

The entrance was completely blocked by a chainlink gate. I hadn't been there in years. I'd forgotten about this. The gate was overgrown with several seasons of vines and weeds. When Dan and I had used the entrance, it was open to anyone. However, about ten years back the city council had ordered the caves sealed. This "considered and unanimous action in the greater public interest" came after two out-of-state kids had fallen and died in the caves. Well, they weren't the first. If you didn't know what you were doing, the caves of Darkhorse were definitely dangerous. At least a dozen people had croaked in them over the years. I thought the city fathers had over-reacted by blocking the entrance. Bureaucrats tend to over-do or under-do almost everything. They didn't ask my opinion, though, and I didn't offer it. I had the urge, but I was afraid that if I spoke up, my old experiences with Dan would come out. Then who knew what kind of official questions I'd have to face. It wasn't for me. Joe Smith preferred a low profile.

I pulled away most of the weeds to get a better look at the gate. It was secured with a rusty old Master combination lock. I jerked it a couple of times, but it held. Then I noticed that the top hinge had pulled away from the cement seal against the cave rock to the left. By bracing myself and working at it, I was gradually able to bend the gate down enough to squeeze through. On the other side, I brushed the dust and weed seeds from my coat and pants. I turned on my miner's light and trudged into the caves.

Dan had told me to meet him at the ring. I knew the way by heart. I'd been there literally a thousand times. For several years, I'd gone into Darkhorse almost once a day, hoping to find Dan. That may seem stupid to you, and I can see why. After all, even search and rescue pros tend to give up after a week or two. This was different. You see, I always had the unshakable feeling that Dan might be alive. A slim hope, true. Highly irrational? Probably. But Dan was special. Not only did he break the IQ scales, but he and I knew something that no one else did about the Darkhorse caves. They weren't entirely natural. I don't mean supernatural. That crap is for the crystal worshippers and cult crawlers. No, what I mean is that there were things in Darkhorse that were man made and shouldn't have been there. The ring, for instance. I thought it was barely possible that Dan had slipped into someplace—a doorway I'd never found, perhaps—or was taken by someone. In one of his wilder moments, Dan had speculated that one section of the caves might be a gateway into alternate realities. We had ample cause to wonder about that, because whenever we went all the way through the caves, things were—well, *different*. Subtle things. Like a missing letter in the alphabet. People you knew with the wrong color hair. Buildings that weren't in the town a few hours earlier, or stores with strange tenants. At first we wondered if we were going a little crazy. It didn't feel crazy, though. Not exactly. It did and it didn't. The events were weird, but we didn't seem screwed up inside or to each other.

There was also the overwhelmingly solid fact that we never found our families again. Oh, we found people who were close, people who resembled our moms and dads, but there was always something eerily *off*. Something that didn't ring true. We'd deeply, badly lost our way in life. Or some kind of science we didn't understand had played very nasty games with us.

In any case, I never found my way back to my original home, or reality, or whatever you choose to call it. Finally, I had to settle down and make something of myself. I'd picked Lebanon—or this version of it—partly because there had never been someone like me in the town. There was no risk of running into a near double or his kin. I'd had close calls with that several times. I didn't know if anything bad would happen, but it was an uncomfortable feeling and it would certainly call attention to me. I didn't want that.

It feels lame putting it into words in this cheap little digital recorder. Hell, maybe, as Dan used to say, we'd stumbled into some kind of dimensional gate. Sounds goofy, doesn't it? Remember, though, that we were only about 15 at the time and had probably watched way too many episodes of *The Outer Limits* and Saturday night horror shows.

Who had made the things under Darkhorse? Like the ring or the steel-lined geyser? Well, we never found out about that, either. We suspected that it was connected to a US Army project. After all, there was an oddball base up on the back side of the butte. It had been built in a flurry of hurry back in the eighties, all hush-hush and no contact with the local folks. It had long since been abandoned. Or nearly so. Just a skeleton military police staff, patrolling the miles-long, 14-foot high, razor-wired perimeter fence day and night. They brooked no nonsense from trespass attempts. Dan himself had almost gotten caught spying on the base from a giant fir tree.

It was stranger than a barking cat. The Army never told anyone what the base was for or why it was still minimally maintained. Town gossip held that not even the state governor knew. Or if he did, he never said. Now and then some young reporter would get interested for awhile, but his inquiry would die on the vine. Traffic in and out of the base was skimpy. When it existed, it was always by helicopter, the noiseless, stealthy types. Private citizen inquiries about the place were diverted to the Pentagon in Washington, D.C. I knew, because I'd tried. The Pentagon would say—ever so politely—that the base was there "for national security purposes." That's all anyone ever found out. Or at least that's all they publicly admitted.

Now, though, if Dan was alive, maybe I'd get some answers after these many years. More than anything, I realized, it was the prospect of hard, straight answers that had drawn me down into Darkhorse again. Maybe the answers would stop my nightmares. I figured that just seeing Dan alive ought to help do that.

I made good time descending the several levels of the cave system. I took all the correct turns. Nothing had changed. It was exactly as I'd remembered it: a maze of old magma vents shot through with limestone caverns and channels. At 5:55 I passed through the "howler." That was a cavern with a mysterious steel-lined, irregular geyser that went off with a forlorn moaning sound, like an animal being tortured. I quickly passed through the section and entered a long, up-sloping tunnel. It was thick with steam. At six o'clock I arrived at what we called the ring.

I looked around. No one was there, but the ring looked the same as I remembered it. A few inches wide, it rimmed the tunnel in a perfect circle. The metal was iridescent, giving off rainbow colors in the dim light. I ran my fingers over the surface. Despite the steam, no condensation ever formed on this metal, whatever it was.

"Hey, ol' bud," a deep voice said behind me.

I flinched. The hair on my arms and legs stood up, like I'd passed close to a big power transformer. It was Dan's voice. Maybe a bit more gravely, but it was the same deep sound he'd had since he was fourteen.

I slowly turned to look at him, a smile forming on my face.

There was a strange light behind him. It threw his face into black shadow.

"Dan?" I squinted and asked, my voice cracking. "Is it really you?"

"It's me," he said.

Then he raised a gun and shot me.

There was a little dart lodged in my chest. I looked at it stupidly for a second, then felt my eyes roll up into my head as everything spun into darkness.

Chapter 11

Consciousness came back in bits and pieces.

I smelled a combination of rubbing alcohol and electrical insulation. I sensed no light or sound. The odor of fresh cotton sheets came into olfactory focus next. It was followed by a whiff of chlorine. Then a fuzzy light and a low humming sound snapped into my awareness almost at the same time. I felt no heat, no cold, no pressure. I couldn't feel my own body and couldn't move. I didn't care. Contentment filled me. I drifted in and out with only a few sources of input, like a primitive animal that hadn't fully evolved.

After awhile, the light sharpened into an overhead lamp. I studied the fixture, but it didn't register. I knew it was a light, but I didn't know why it was there. Next, the humming sound gained edges: a hiss, a regular ping, a slight roar. Finally, floating up out of unconsciousness, everything clicked into conceptual focus.

I was in a small room, lit overhead by a fluorescent lamp. The noise came from an air conditioner duct set high on the right wall. I was in a bed. I was strapped tight around my arms, torso, and legs. The straps were white with large chrome buckles. My head was free. I could raise it slightly and move from side to side. I could feel my body again. I could move everything important.

I couldn't remember much. Squeezing through the entrance gate of Darkhorse was my last, cogent memory.

Except for a slight headache, nothing seem to hurt. Okay, I

thought. Guess I haven't been injured. At least not badly.

About ten feet beyond the foot of my bed was a door. There were no windows to the room, but I couldn't be sure because I couldn't see behind me.

After awhile, I began to feel thirsty. I tried to yell, but produced only a squawk. My throat was as dry as a parched leaf. I worked my tongue around my mouth and finally got enough saliva to swallow once.

"Hey!" I yelled, my voice rough and raspy. "Anyone? What's going on? Anybody hear me?"

A female voice came from a speaker grill I hadn't noticed next to the door.

"Please stay calm. Someone will be with you in a minute."

"Who—? Hey! Where am I?"

"In a minute, please."

The voice sounded familiar, but not entirely comforting.

I rested my head. That slight effort had been extraordinarily draining. My temples began to throb. I felt like I was developing a bad hangover.

I must have said it aloud, because the next thing I heard was, "You are!"

It was Dan. He walked into view from behind me. Apparently there was another entrance to the room. I looked him over. It was him all right. He was gray-haired and balding. However, it was his grin, his voice, his build—only slightly heavier than I remembered. He'd always been bigger than me by several inches and thirty pounds. His mom and dad had both been big-boned and strong. He stood the way he used to, with his head slightly cocked and one dark eyebrow raised.

"How ya doing, ol' bud?" he asked.

"Uh, okay, I guess." I felt myself responding to his grin. "Good to see you."

"Yeah, me too. Let me unfasten these straps so I can shake your hand."

He did. His grip was strong, but I noticed that his palm was damp.

He helped me sit up and steadied me as several waves of

dizziness came and went.

After a minute or two, he propped me up in bed with a couple pillows and pulled over a chair. He rested his hands on his knees. He was smiling slightly, but seemed fidgety.

"What gives, Dan?" I asked. "You look like the dog that just got caught with the Thanksgiving turkey."

He looked away for a moment and muttered, "Well, something like that."

"Any water around here?"

"Huh? Oh, sure!"

He seemed grateful for something to do. He jumped to the door's intercom and said, "Lois, get a pitcher of water in here on the double, okay? The subject is as parched as a pony in the Mojave. A couple of Anacins, too. He's got a pounder."

"The subject? I'm a *subject*? Dan, what's going on? Was I in an accident or something?"

Dan shook his head, glanced at me, then looked away. Yeah, he looked guilty about something.

Lois, a pert, dark-haired woman in a nurse's uniform, came in. She put the water and the Anacin on the stainless steel hospital table beside me, nodded at Dan, then turned to leave. As she moved away from Dan, she winked at me and smiled.

"When are you going to ask me out again, Eddie?" she prodded mischievously.

"Not now, Lois, for Pete's sake!" Dan said.

Lois left, still smiling.

What was that about?

Dan poured water and helped me drink. I choked twice. Eventually, I got a half a glass inside me without choking, along with two of the Anacins.

"Crap," I said, "you'd think I'd never done this before." I wiped some water off my chin with the back of my hand. My arm felt heavy and weak. "Might as well be an invalid."

Dan set the glass down, then sat back in his chair, twisting his hands in his lap.

"Well, you kind of are an invalid," he said. "Just not the usual type."

"Huh?"

"Oh, man," he said, closing his eyes. "Well, I guess it's time."

"Dan, you're not making sense."

"Yeah, I know." He met my eyes. "It's time to tell you what's going on."

"Be kinda nice," I agree. "This is pretty weird."

"More than you ever imagined."

"We never had any secrets, did we?"

"Oh, we had a few. Anyway, I did," he said. "In fact, that's as good a place as any to start explaining. With the secrets, I mean. You see, your—" He stopped abruptly, like he was choking down a sob.

"Dan? Jeez, are you okay?"

The Dan I remembered was never *this* emotional. But then, people change in 30 years.

He nodded, swallowed, and continued, "Your whole life's been a secret, ol' bud. One, big, ugly, monster of a secret. Even from you. At least that's how it's going to seem to you for a little while yet."

I looked at him blankly.

"What does that mean?"

Dan rubbed his eyes and said, "I've dreaded this day. Guess there's no way to deal with it except up and at 'em."

He pulled a small recorder out of his pocket and turned it on. I heard my own voice. It was a copy of the account I'd made a few weeks earlier. In it, I'd started trying to explain how we'd found the caves, got lost in them, lost each other. The whole ball of wax. Therapy, I guess the psychologists would call it. Self-help, highly improvised. But somewhere in the back of my mind, I'd also had a notion of hiding the tape. The truth, the little bit I knew of it, seemed to have a will of its own. It wanted out of the dark jail cell I'd jammed it into so many years ago.

"How'd you get that?" I asked, both surprised and irritated, and a touch chagrined.

I hadn't given the recording to anyone. As far as I'd known, it was in my room, tucked in the back of my sock drawer.

"I, uh, that is, the Army got it."

"The Army," I said.

Maybe this was a whopper of another nightmare. If it was, I appeared to be in too deep to get out of it. Besides, it was getting interesting. I wanted to know what happened next. I reached down and pinched myself. It hurt.

Dan smiled, catching the action.

"Oh, it's real," he said. "You're real. This is real." He waved at the room. "It's all so real I'd like to—well, never mind what I'd like to do. That's all irrelevant."

I closed my eyes and said, "I take it the Army was spying on me? Why? There's no reason for—"

"There's *always* a reason!" Dan snapped. "Damn it, didn't I teach you that?"

His face was red.

"Sure, sure. Yeah, right, Dan. You did. Calm down."

This was not the always-in-control Dan I remembered. Stress oozed from his pores like rancid sweat.

He rubbed his face twice with both hands.

"Sorry. Okay, let me give it another go. The cave stuff? Most of it didn't happen."

"Huh?"

"Oh, we went in there, all right. But only once. Not dozens of times before I got lost. You didn't go in there a thousand times like you think, either. Just once."

He held up a meaty index finger to emphasize the point.

"But, Dan, I distinctly remember that—"

"No!" he shouted. Almost instantly, he softened his voice, holding a hand up, palm out, as though stopping traffic. "No, ol' bud, you don't remember. You think you do, but you don't. False memories. The Army implanted them."

"Hell, Dan," I said, "I'm not that uneducated. It's not possible to implant false memories in such detail."

He smiled bitterly.

"That's what the general public believes. But it is with a device called an mnemonic imprinter, an MI. It's pronounced 'me,' like the musical note. They've had crude versions of the darn things for almost 40 years. As the telecosm revolution combined with genetic engineering advances, they got better and better. Using the breakthroughs of DNA-based encryption and robotic software agents, it became possible to code artificial digital information directly onto memory cells. Actually, onto new cells generated from the brain's own basic stem cell supply. The stem cells naturally migrate into their proper locations taking the artificial memories with them."

I rubbed my eyes with my thumbs, then let out a long sigh.

"Dan, I'm latching onto only about half of what you're saying."

"Huh? Oh, sorry. I assumed that maybe you were a lot farther along."

"Why would I be? I was never interested in science the way you were."

Dan snorted, as though I'd told a stupid joke.

"Yeah, right. Well, never mind. Suffice it to say that the MIs have gotten so good in recent years that you can't tell the implanted memories from the real ones. No one can. In fact, they can use the MI's electronic and chemical functions to totally suppress real memories. That makes the false ones stand out even sharper. The MIs were first developed during the late Cold War in order to turn Soviet spies and send them back with phony information. Even under truth serums, the MI implants held up. Hell, they're so good now that they can create what are called virtual personalities. You've got one. It's replaced your original. You aren't who you think you are. You didn't do what you think you did."

He sunk his face back into his hands and groaned. I heard him mumble, "How'd I ever get into this? Surely there was a better way."

Then he looked back up, tears streaming down his normally stolid face and said, "I'm so sorry. But I had no other choice. I really didn't."

He took a moment to pull a couple tissues off the box by my bed and blow his nose.

"You see, " he continued, "you had something in your brain

that we couldn't let out. You knew too much and we couldn't risk letting you run around free. To put it bluntly, we enslaved you in the name of preserving liberty. Your loss was the country's gain. Or at least it was, until the Russians stole it."

I laughed. It started as a chuckle and kept getting bigger. I couldn't help it. It was too much. It was absurd, and I'd suddenly seen an explanation that made sense. This was a gigantic hoax. It had to be. It was the only thing that made sense. It was coming back to me now. Dan had been famous for his practical jokes. He'd always been a good actor, too.

"Wipe the thespian tears away, Dan," I said. "This takes the prize. One of your best performances. I gotta hand it to you, you had me going, you did."

He was shaking his head in apparent frustration.

"No! You have to believe me!" he protested.

"Aw, come on, Dan," I said, my amusement turning into annoyance. "Enough's enough. Drop the act. You've had your fun. How'd I get here? *Really*."

"It's no damned joke!" He slammed his right palm on the arm of his chair as he said it, half rising and glaring at me.

I looked back at him for a long moment. Well, maybe it wasn't an act after all. At least I was willing to accept that Dan believed what he was saying, as cockamamie as it sounded.

"Uh, well, sure. Don't bust a brain vein, Dan. Let's take it one thing at a time. You say this MI device replaced my memories with false ones. Effectively an entire false *life* since I was fifteen—is that what you're claiming?"

"Yes!" he cried, leaping up and pacing the room. "Yes, exactly, that's it!"

I frowned in confusion.

"But Dan, I'm *nobody*. You're the guy that got the mental steroids, not me. I've always been an ordinary Joe."

"Yeah, that's what you're calling yourself now, isn't it? Joe?"

"Good as any."

"Well, your real name is Eddie Jones. Didn't you hear Lois call you that? And you've got everything backwards."

"What?"

"You know how you've always thought I was the one with the IQ that soared out past Saturn?"

"Yeah," I said carefully. "It's pretty obvious which of us had it and which of us didn't."

"It's obvious to your *false* memories, Eddie. But it's not true."

"What the hell are you talking about?"

"Ol' bud, realize that *you* are the one with the high-test brain pan, not me."

All I could come up with was, "Bull. I know smart when I see it. You've got it. I don't."

Dan paced around for a few seconds, then leaned up against the wall by the door and smiled, shaking his head slowly, but a bit sadly.

He said, "No, it was always you. Never me. All those fancy books and magazines you thought I read. All those great grades you thought I got in school. All the scrambling by universities around the country to court me into their programs. None of that was me. It was you. The MI machine turned it around. Had to."

"I don't feel that smart, Dan. If I am, what am I doing here? If I'm that smart, how'd you catch me? And how come I can't think my way out of a tissue box?"

"It's the MI's suppression effects. There's still a chip implanted under your skin at the back of your skull."

I reached back, probing, trying to feel anything abnormal under my skin.

"Oh, you can't feel it. It's too deep, up under the bone. But it's there. It electronically suppresses your true memories. We permanently deactivated it, but the transition to a normal state takes time. You haven't shaken your virtual personality yet. As you do, you'll feel your intelligence return. When it does, it's going to crash into you like a wave. However, it'll take a few hours. Right now, I figure you're functioning at about—oh, roughly one-half of normal. About equal to me. Know what my IQ is, Eddie?"

I just looked at him.

"135. Not quite a genius, but no retard, either. Think about it. You're in this hospital bed, all buzzed up with electronic fog, and your brain is already working as well as mine. I know it is, because there's an artificial intelligence program monitoring our conversation and it's good at estimating this stuff."

He stepped closer and held up the face of a wristwatch so I could see. It wasn't a wristwatch, but a miniature video screen. Dan said it was linked by ultraviolet beam to a computer outside the room. The screen read, "E. Jones IQ running index: 142." As I watched, the number jumped to 148, then to 153. It looked very impressive.

I swore and said, "Big deal. Anyone can jury-rig a number cruncher like that. It's a toy! Hell, I could do it myself with a safety pin, spit, and a calculator watch."

Dan smiled and said, "I couldn't. Could you really?"

"Sure, it's just a matter of altering a few parameters by blocking the tunneling of an ion through the—"

I stopped.

"Dan, what did I just start to say?" I asked

"You got me, Eddie. But you sounded serious."

"I was. But I don't have any right to be! I'm me, plain old Joe Smith. The gray man. The average, anonymous guy who lives in an out-of-the-way apartment in a small town and damned well likes it."

"No, you're not," Dan said. "You're about as average as Einstein—except less so. You're also one stubborn, bull-headed maverick. Which is why we eventually had to put you under the MI."

Just then, Lois the nurse walked in and said sternly to Dan, "General Davis, you have to let him rest now or you'll risk his recovery. He's in a delicate state."

"*General* Davis?" I asked weakly. I felt the prick of something on my right arm and was woozily aware of a needle being extracted from me and Lois smiling sympathetically.

Chapter 12

When I came up out of it, things were happening faster. This time I wasn't strapped in. When Lois entered, I was trying to stand up, but feeling shaky.

"I supposed you're going to tell me I shouldn't try this," I said accusingly.

"Not at all," she said. "The sooner you get up and get the blood moving, the better off you'll be. And the sooner you can take me to dinner."

I looked her over. "I know you?"

"You better. We were getting pretty serious before this MI mess interrupted everything. Need any help getting dressed? You've got an appointment in about ten minutes."

I looked down at myself. I was stark naked, but Lois didn't seem to notice. Or maybe she'd seen it many times before. She caught my eye and winked, then helped me into shorts and socks and a crisp, beige coverall. She dropped a pair of canvas shoes on the floor and I stepped into them. Everything fit. I ran a hand over my jaw. I felt clean and my face was shaved.

"I took care of all that before you woke up," she said perkily. It was a nice kiss.

"How do I look?" I asked.

"For a recovering lug, not bad. C'mon. Let's go for a tour."

She took my arm and led me out. Her grip was not particularly nurse-like and her hip periodically brushed mine. I could smell a light perfume. I'd smelled it before.

The door to my room opened into a plain hallway painted

industrial gray. We took a right and then a left and entered a huge cavern. The floor was a maze of partitioned rooms and small buildings, interspersed with various kinds of machinery. A bank of bright metal halide lamps on the cavern ceiling lit everything to daylight intensity.

"The Army base," I said under my breath. "The real one."

Lois merely nodded. Dan approached from around a corner, accompanied by another man. Both wore Army uniforms. Dan's had two stars, while the other fellow's had three.

"Feeling better?" Dan asked, shaking my hand.

"Yeah, as a matter of fact, I am."

I took the other man's hand and asked, "And you are?"

"General Ned Jefferson. I run this show. Good to have you with us again, Dr. Jones."

I looked at Dan. "*Doctor* Jones?"

Dan nodded.

General Jefferson smiled and said, "Afraid so. Doctorates in eight fields, isn't that right, Dan?"

"Nine, actually," Dan said.

"I don't recollect anything of the kind," I said mulishly.

Jefferson chuckled and clapped me on the back, "Oh, you will. Believe me, you will. Just takes a little time. Meanwhile, let's see if you recognize anything in this joint. You used to work here."

He and Dan led me down into the warren, indicating various features. Oddly, not much surprised me. When they pointed to something, I usually knew what they were talking about. I spotted a compact structure off to one side.

"Hmmm," I said. "A miniaturized fusion reactor based on the Vasili Armanov design from around 1980. I thought they'd abandoned that when that Bose-Einsteinian condensate trick came on line and they were able to suspend hydrogen atoms with the—"

I stopped cold, hearing my words from their point of view.

"How do I know that?" I asked. "I don't remember learning anything about it."

Jefferson laughed and said, "You know it and a thousand

times more than you *know* you know right now."

"The reactor must be the source of the steam," I observed. "You heat water for power and vent it through the howler geyser. The caves act as a big steam suppresser, masking your output from the outside."

"Bingo," Jefferson said. "Actually, we vent it through several places like that. That particular howler is the only one you've seen. You look a bit peaked, son. Let's find some java jolt and sit down a spell. We need to talk. The psyche boys say that the more we can prod your memory like this, the faster it'll recover."

We entered a small cafeteria. There were two workers sitting at a table, but when Jefferson nodded curtly at them, they left. Jefferson and I took a table while Dan got us coffee.

"Black for Ned and me," Dan said. "You still like yours with creamer, Eddie?"

"Yeah, no sugar," I replied automatically.

"Well, now," Jefferson said after we'd had a chance to sip our brew, "let me shoot this shell straight out of the cannon. Dr. Jones, you are a unique individual. Probably the most special mind that old Mama Nature has yet offered the human race. Bar none."

"Humph," I said. "From where I sit Mama has plenty of work to do."

"You always were a recalcitrant bastard. Give the cynicism a rest, son. Listen a spell, okay?"

I nodded warily and held my coffee with both hands. The warmth was comforting.

"Back in the '80s," Jefferson began, "you were a 15-year-old whelp with a major ax to grind. You didn't grow up in Lebanon, but in Los Angeles, California."

"But—"

"No buts. That's what happened. You were an orphan. We figure your parents abandoned you about the time you were 11, or maybe you just ran away. You lived by your wits and somehow had sense enough to learn to read and stay out of gangs. You were a loner then, as you are now. We didn't have to fake that part with the MI machine. Hard to do, actually. It's a core of your personality. Core stuff is stubborn, so we worked around it. Anyway, at fifteen you got arrested for felony theft."

"I tried to hold up a bank," I interrupted. "I got over $70,000 but had the rotten luck to run into an off-duty cop on my way out the door."

"Ah," Dan said, "more memories seep under the door."

"That little incident landed you in court," Jefferson said. "Lucky for you, you got a sympathetic judge. It was your first offense of any kind. At least the first that was officially recorded. The judge dickered with the D.A. and they cut a deal. If you agreed to be tested and go through high school, she'd keep you out of the slammer."

"Hmmm, I don't remember that," I said, frustration lacing my words.

Jefferson held up his hand, "Patience, patience. Don't fight it, son. Let it come in its own time. That's how these things work. The process is uneven and unpredictable, but it does work. You taught us that."

"I taught you?"

Jefferson looked at Dan and asked, "You didn't tell him?"

Dan shook his head.

"Tell what?" I asked.

"The MI machine we used on you? It was your invention. Oh, there had been crude devices before it, but you were the one to finally turn it into something that was a precision instrument. The full name of the MI machine is the Jones Mnemonic Implant Device. J-MID for short. Or just MI. Shorter slang has a way of taking over."

"Slang drives out formal," I said.

"Pardon?" Jefferson asked.

"A play on the old economic monetary dictum that bad money drives out good. Say's Law, it's called."

"Ah," Jefferson said. "Well, that's neither here nor there. Once they got you into the school system, they ran you through the IQ and other appraisal tests and, Lord above, guess what they found?"

"I had brains."

"Not just brains. You were one *gawdawfully* smart little pecker. Hell, son, you were the brightest fellow they'd ever tested in the state of California. Not merely of your age group. Ever. Of any age group. Then some bureaucrat started comparing records and found that no one in the whole country had ever tested as high as you did. Oh, there were plenty of people with more knowledge in their heads and innumerable with superior experience. Your brain pan was filled with tons of trivia and no more organized than a couple of cats in a water barrel."

"Sorry," I said. "That's all a fog upstairs."

"Uh-huh. Normal. When it comes, be ready for a tsunami. It tends to flood in all at once. You proved it with some formula you called 'synthetic fractal consciousness.' Not my field. I take the lab boys' word for it."

I looked up at the ceiling, remembering, "Synthetic fractal consciousness is the theory that the human mind stores memories and concepts in endlessly divisible, electro-chemical fractal patterns. The virtue of the system is that it can keep information organized when necessary, but also stimulate the chaos required for intuitive leaps. The fractals are not just two-dimensional, but multidimensional, making it possible for end-points to fold and touch in countless combinations, thereby making unexpected connections. The theory refutes the notions of Ray Kurzweil *et al* that the brain is essentially a rapidly downloadable, predictable pattern. It's why no one's been able to artificially duplicate a human mind. And, I might add, probably never will. I invented that?"

Jefferson nodded, grinning from ear to ear. He swigged down about half his coffee, grunted, and continued, "Anyway, back to your education days. Then, as now, Uncle Sam's service boys had ways of spotting anyone whose IQ topped 140. That's technically the demarcation point of genius. Well, your name got flagged in neon lights and fireworks. Through various and devious means, the Army snapped you up for the good of the country."

"Sounds like conscription to me," I shot back with some vehemence, surprising myself, "I don't believe in it. It's immoral, impractical, too."

"Maybe so. I'll leave it to the ethical specialists. But from this ol' grunt's point of view, your choices were thinner than Saran wrap, son. Besides, at every step of the way, we gave you an option out. Conscriptees don't get that option. You don't remember it yet. You will, though. And you'll see that I was telling you the truth."

"Or it'll be another elaborate false memory. How will I know the difference?"

"Dr. Jones," Jefferson said, leaning forward on his elbows, "the MI has its limitations. It has a nature as does any other machine. It is constrained by that nature. We can only get so elaborate with it or the whole thing falls apart. That's why we had to create a false personality for you. It's why we had to keep it fairly dull and simple. Now, you can believe that or not. Right now, it doesn't seem dull and simple, but rich and complicated. That's how a virtual personality is supposed to appear from the inside. However, once your brain kicks back into the stratosphere, you won't question what I'm saying. You'll see it in an instant. The MI world will fade and you'll see it for just how artificial it was. Believe me, son, the detail of reality far supersedes anything the virtual reality geeks can create."

"So you say."

"Feet dug in as deep as ever," he said to Dan.

Dan sipped his coffee.

"Anyway, we got you into an Army academy," Jefferson went on. "This was a special place. The Army created it just for you. We had to. We'd never had an asset like you."

"Asset? I was an asset?"

Jefferson nodded. "Absolutely. A hell of a monster asset. You were something completely new. Your capacity for abstraction, your intuitive leaps, your creativity — they were boundless. And fast? God, you were a fast S.O.B.! You see, using DNA/MF—"

"MF?"

"Uh, mitochondrial forensics, I believe. Using that, we discovered a mighty interesting thing. You were the bastard son of an unusual *family*. As a matter of fact, you have a half brother in the Space Command. His name is Kevin Jones. What makes this guy special, what makes your whole family unusual, is a thing called the Slowdown. Tell him about it, Dan."

Dan looked at his hands and said, "It's an inborn trait which allows these folks—the men, anyway, because it doesn't appear to show up in the women, and, no, we don't know why— it allows them to suddenly go into a kind of physical hyperdrive. To them, everything else slows to a fraction of normal speed. It's kind of like what some athletes describe when they're 'in the groove' and everything seems easy."

"But if it's in the normal realm—"

"In your case, it's a several times greater effect. Things don't actually slow down for you, of course. You are just moving very fast. Trouble is, in your family's version, they don't have control over it. It only kicks in when they are in mortal danger. Using this skill, your half brother actually saved President Washington's life at a big banquet right after the Engels Extension conflict."

"Well," I said, hearing my voice cut deep with sarcasm, "I've noticed about as much speed in my physical skills as a slug on snow. Maybe you have the wrong guy."

Jefferson growled and Dan shook his head.

"We don't have the wrong guy, Eddie," Dan said. "You know enough to understand that this DNA technology today is next to foolproof. The odds of us being wrong are astronomical. Forget it."

Jefferson finished his coffee and handed his cup to Dan. "Get me another, if you will. All this yakkin' is drying me out."

Dan got us fresh coffee and Jefferson continued the story.

"We absolutely, positively, overnight delivery *don't* have the wrong guy," he said. "It's just that your talent didn't show up the same way the other Jones' did. Yours showed up entirely in the mental arena. You were born with a kind of intellectual Slowdown. Better still, you could turn it on and off at *will*. We figure that explains how you survived without so much as a scratch all those years alone on the streets. You simply ran brain-circles around your opposition."

"But of course the Army couldn't use an undisciplined delinquent," Dan chimed in. "You had a super brain, but you had only rudimentary organizational skills."

"It's often said by those who hate the services that military intelligence is an oxymoron," Jefferson said. "Hell, even a lot of non-intelligence service guys say it! But it's not true. The Army and the other services, too, have more than their share of bright guys. There are a hell of a lot of them working in the field of conceptual enhancement, dedicated to discovering how men think, what works best, and how to teach it. Highly practical-oriented stuff. We threw every expert we had at you and you absorbed their knowledge like a black hole sucking up spare stardust."

Dan nodded at me, trying to reinforce Jefferson's pitch.

"You see," Dan said, giving me a wide-eyed look, "you were, and are, so far above a normal genius that you make him seem downright retarded."

"Actually," Jefferson said, "the tests showed that you made a normal genius appear to be the equivalent of a highly intelligent dog."

I stared at both of them in a mixture of disbelief and astonishment. This was too strange.

"We think," General Jefferson said slowly, "that the Lord is trying something new with you."

"If there is a God," I said.

"Maybe there is, maybe not. I believe it and it gives me comfort to believe it. But I don't profess to be a theology expert. Anyway, this isn't the place to argue the subject. This we know, Dr. Jones: there's never been anything like you on the planet. Not to our knowledge."

"Nice to be special," I said.

"Mouthy little bastard, as always," Jefferson shot back.

"So what's wrong with being different?" I asked. "Too much trouble for Army regulations?"

"It's worse than that, Eddie," Dan added, "or better, depending on your perspective. The studies that the psyche boys have done suggest something even more profound."

"I'm about profounded out," I said, feeling embarrassed by the outlandish attention. I was either hearing the wildest story of my life, or I was already in a padded room somewhere hallucinating continuously.

"I imagine so," Dan replied. "But what the studies indicate is that you are the first of your line."

"Beg pardon?"

"Let me put it in Biblical terms," Jefferson interjected. "Eddie, you are the Adam of the next stage of human evolution. That makes you more than a national asset. It makes you an asset of mankind."

At that point, I fainted.

Chapter 13

When I awoke the next morning, Dan was again beside me. "Hi," he said. "Lois says you probably keeled over yesterday from lack of food. We got you up and completely forgot to give you breakfast. Didn't let you drink any water, either. Plus, the coffee probably dehydrated you further. Sorry."

"I feel okay now," I said, getting up and getting dressed. "By the way, I'm nobody's asset."

"What?"

"Before I fainted yesterday, that Jefferson character said I was an asset of mankind. That sounds suspiciously like I'm not much more than a slave."

"Oh, I don't think he meant it that way," Dan said.

I raised an eyebrow as I slipped on my shoes. "You don't *think* so, eh? Well, I have a somewhat different impression of the good general."

"He let you run loose awhile."

"Yeah, well, that was when he thought I was sweet, dumb, and happy. By the way, why did you guys turn the MI loose on me in the first place?"

"Two reasons," Dan said, almost sheepishly. "You knew too much and you were going rogue on us."

"Going rogue?"

"You were threatening to violate your clearances. You disagreed with some of our projects and intended to go to the press with your moaning and groaning. It was either the MI or permanent incarceration. You should thank Jefferson, Eddie.

He gave you a second chance. He figured that after you came out of the MI's effects, you might straighten out. I told him you would. I went to bat for you. So tell me, *will* you fly right?"

"Depends," I said. "Depends on how effectively you convince me I should. Let me ask you this, Dan. There must have been something paramount, some project that my so-called roguishness threatened more than others. What was it?"

From the open doorway, General Jefferson said, "It had to do with the AM guns."

"The what?"

"Remember the antimatter guns that the Russians used on us in the Third World War?"

"Whoa, hold on!" I said. "From what I read in the media, it was the Russians who invented those things. Not us."

"You invented them," Dan said flatly. "Way back in 1990, when you were in your twenties. But then during the big Energy Department espionage scandal of the Clinton years, some idiot sold the data on the sly to the Rooskies. We were cooperating with Energy at the time, but they were in charge of overall security. Their security was pathetic—at least from the viewpoint of the Army, especially by today's standards. We knew it and pleaded with Energy to tighten their hatches, but politics prevented us from doing much about it. We didn't discover the AM theft until years later, after WW3 was over. Some lower DoE official finally tipped us. We'd built only a couple of table-top prototypes of the weapon; right here in these caverns, as a matter of fact. We intended to save the concept for future use. We had plenty of other stuff coming on line, you see, and we didn't figure we'd need it for a long, long time. No one in the services dreamt that we were on the verge of facing the exact thing wielded by the Russians. Oh, the Rooskies were good. They kept their theft secret, up to and including trying to blackmail the world into submission. Classic deception, and it fooled the horse-pucky out of us. Almost Pearl Harbor all over again—doubled and squared."

"Know your enemy and use secret agents to good avail, I believe some Chinese strategist once said," I observed.

"Well, you have to remember the context, Dr. Jones," Jefferson said. "After Yeltsin's resignation and the Chaos Years, after Russia went Soviet again, it was almost impossible to run decent intelligence over there. It just got by us."

"Where did I come in?"

"Uh, well," Dan said, "you thought we should have fielded the antimatter weapons right away, back in the early '90s. You thought we were irresponsible not to have done so. You anticipated the Russian theft and the subsequent attack. We didn't believe you. We *couldn't* believe you."

Dan glanced at Jefferson, as though seeking permission. Dan looked back at me.

"You see, Eddie, you'd designed something that intelligence agencies had dreamt about for decades, but had never believed possible. You developed a theft forecasting program. You derived it from some overlooked customer order-flow software used in the shipping industry to predict inventory requirements, then combined it with several arcane elements of gaming theory snipped out of the entertainment business, and then—"

"Okay, okay," I said impatiently. These guys seemed to take *forever* to say anything. I felt like they were on downers while I was on speed. "I woofed and wowed and forecast a war and some thievery, then got pissed when you wouldn't believe me. How did that justify your mashing my brains with the MI machine like you did?"

"Son, I thought it was obvious. You threatened to go public with your views. It would have blown our strategy. Worse, it would have blown the existence of this establishment."

"Which is what, exactly?" I asked. "Some kind of adjunct of the Defense Advanced Research Projects Agency?"

"Beyond that, son," Jefferson said. "More adventurous, more willing to tackle far-out ideas, and plenty of them. We're to DARPA what DARPA is to the regular service."

"Why put it here? Why this out-of-the-way place in Oregon, of all places?"

"Why do you think? Didn't you answer your own question, son? The known test areas and labs are the last place you want something like this. Every reporter and conspiracy nut and foreign agent is watching those places."

I nodded slowly, feeling a little foggy again, "Yeah, sure, I guess you're right."

"Eddie, there's something else we haven't told you about this high-track brain you've got," Dan said.

"Which is?"

"It's unstable. Or at least it used to be. See, you go along fine for awhile, then suddenly your emotions go into warp drive and you get paranoid. In the years before we put you through the MI, we had to physically subdue and sedate you quite a number of times. Back then, your outbursts were limited to mild violence. Throwing plates; pushing people around a little; breaking chairs. Considering all you were producing, inventing, and improving, we could put up with tantrums. But when you threatened to go public and break your clearances, well, we couldn't allow it."

"Hmmm," I said. I forced myself to smile thinly, "sounds like I was an asshole."

"You were," Jefferson said. "Grade A."

"Uh, look, I hate to break up this data dump, but can I get some food?" I asked. "I'm starting to feel a little light-headed."

Over breakfast, wolfing down eggs, bacon, ham, orange juice, and English muffins slathered in blackberry jam, I pointed a fork at General Jefferson and asked, "What I still don't get is the time frame on all of this. According to my internal clock, I lost track of Dan in these caves something like twenty-eight years ago, give or take. But you hinted yesterday that I'd only been under the MI's influence for a few years."

"Truthfully, son, it's been under two years. And I'm afraid Dan lied to you. You two never explored these caves together. You never lost track of each other. Not even once. That was all phonied up. Part of the deal. It's how the MI works."

"But I remember—"

"Falsely," Dan said.

"What about the ring? How did I know the path through the caves in order to get here a couple days ago?"

"Oh, that's the easiest answer of all; those things never happened," Jefferson said. "You've never left this complex. You've been here throughout the entire MI treatment. Oh, the caves are real, sure. You can see we're in 'em. But what you *think* you remember was merely an elaborately detailed memory constructed with the aid of a man walking the route with a high-rez CCD mini-camera. As I said, the MI incorporates a sophisticated form of digital interfacing with the human brain. You'll recollect the details soon enough. You should. You created that process, too. Or at least the critical parts of it. As to the rest, well, any good Hollywood story editor could have come up with the false memories of your getting lost in the caves, losing Dan, living in an alternate reality, and the whole ball of string. As a matter of fact, two of the people who concocted your MI memories used to work in Hollywood as screenwriters. Amazing what those ratty little freaks can come up with, isn't it?"

"But why such an elaborate thing? Why not come up with something simple?"

"A precaution," Dan said. "In one of your fits, you showed extraordinary adeptness at escape. We barely stopped you. If it had happened again, and you succeeded in getting out of here, we figured that the more ridiculous the story, the more science-fantasy we threw into your pseudo-life, the less chance anyone would listen to you. You'd be just another nutcase wandering the world, yelping for attention. That way, if you tried blabbing secrets in violation of your clearances, you'd be taken no more seriously than the latest UFO abduction fruitcakes. By the way, we *did* work together, you and I. We were friends, even though we didn't grow up together. Heck, we're not even related. That was MI bull, too."

Dan looked ashamed. I think he was. I think he had a conscience. Maybe Jefferson did, too, but if so, he hid it well.

I crunched and swallowed the last of my bacon and settled back with a fresh cup of coffee.

"You called the MI stuff a treatment. Is it supposed to cure my emotional instability? What's the catch? Something's off here, right?"

The two generals looked uncomfortable.

"The catch, if you insist on calling it that," Jefferson said, "is that about half the time the cure procedure doesn't work."

"And if not?"

"You'll eventually revert to the implanted personality of Joe Smith."

"There is no Joe Smith? He's a fake?"

"Yes," said Dan.

"Sooooo," I said, fleshing out the implications, "that means I'll be delusional. Permanently. I'll be living in cuckoo land."

"Essentially," Jefferson said stiffly. "But we'll provide for you. We're not heartless. Think of it as living in a perfect virtual reality, but not knowing it's virtual. You'll forget all this and we'll keep you alive with the best of medical care and nutrition. We'll give you a virtual girlfriend and livelihood and you'll be reasonably happy."

"A hunk of flesh, fed food and fiction, until it dies."

"It's not like that," Dan started to protest.

"The hell it's not!" I said, hissing the words out. I felt the anger rising inside me like a snake uncoiling to strike. I forced it down. I made myself sip some coffee.

"Okay, I see," I said. "And if it works? Then what happens to me?"

"If it works, you're cured," Jefferson said brightly, spreading both hands wide. "You're not the first. From past experience, we know that if you come fully back to your original personality, you will be quite stable from that point on. It's as though the MI life speeds up emotional maturity. You should be fine. Just fine, son."

I nodded and looked back and forth between the two of them. I wondered how many things they hadn't told me.

"If I'm cured, my options will be?"

"To continue your work here, of course," Jefferson said, as though it were obvious.

"What if I don't want to?"

"Huh? But why wouldn't you?"

"Well, for one thing, if your history of my history is true, it sounds like I've spent most of my adult life ensconced in your little government project. Maybe I'd like to see the big wide world. Try something else. Live a little."

"But we thought, with your fantastic brain, that the challenges here would be—"

"Irresistible?"

"Er, yes. I suppose so."

"Maybe you've lived in this high technology goldfish bowl too long, General."

"Hey, now just a minute, that's uncalled for. This crap about military men being nothing but robots to their profession is a lot of thunderclap!"

"It's not a comment on the military," I replied. "It's an observation of living things. Sometimes they like to explore outside their cages."

"It's not a friggin' cage!" Jefferson barked.

"If it's not, then are you saying that if I recover I'm free to go?"

"Yes," Dan said.

"No!" Jefferson contradicted him. "You're too damned valuable, son! The country needs you. You're the first of your kind. You're a whole, new species, don't you get it? Your type may not turn up again for a hundred thousand years. Maybe never. You're the race's *future*. You've got to pass on your genes and—"

He snapped his mouth shut.

"Oh? Sounds like you intend to use me as a stud in some kind of eugenics program, General," I said carefully.

Jefferson got up and went to the coffee machine, barking over his shoulder, "Dan, try to talk some sense into Mr. Genius, will you?"

Dan looked at me and started to speak. "Listen to me, ol' bud, okay?"

"Hold on a second," I said to Dan, vigorously rubbing my face with my hands. "I'm a bit light-headed. My stomach feels like someone filled it with dishwater. I think my breakfast is rebelling."

"You do look a little pale," Dan said, cocking his head and

looking me over.

"I can barely keep my eyes open."

"The pullout process from MI conditioning can be uneven," he noted, reaching for my arm to help me up. "We'd better get you back to your room. You need rest."

"Problem?" Jefferson asked, returning with his coffee, his eyebrows raised in inquiry.

"Dr. Jones doesn't feel so hot. I'm going to get him to bed and have Lois look him over. We certainly don't want a relapse on our hands."

"Certainly not," Jefferson said conjuring up a thin smile. "We've got way too much invested. Besides, I've got duties chewin' at my shoes. Let's call it a day. We'll pick up again tomorrow morning, Dr. Jones. See you here at eight-hundred hours, sharp."

"Yeah, sure," I said weakly, holding both hands over my gut and groaning.

Dan got me settled in my room and then took off, begging other commitments. I figured he probably didn't want to hang around to see what course my stomach rebellion might take. In my memory — such as it was — Dan had always been a bit on the squeamish side.

No more than a minute later, Lois came in.

She approached the bed, put her hands on her hips, and said, "Overloaded you, did they?"

"Maybe," I said warily.

"Uh-huh," she replied, taking my pulse. She put a palm on my forehead, looked closely at my eyes, then stuck a thermometer in my mouth. "Back in three minutes."

"Rigfft," I said over the thermometer.

When she returned, she locked the door behind her.

She read the thermometer, shook it back down, then said, "Hmmm, no fever at all. You're not sweating. Your eyes aren't dilated or bloodshot. Your pulse is normal. Your skin looks and feels fine for a man who's been through what you've endured."

"So?"

She folded her arms and looked at me a long moment. The

corners of her mouth curled slightly upward and she said, "Eddie, if I didn't know better, I'd say you're faking it."

I expressed mild outrage. "Why would I want to do that?"

"You tell me. You're the one with everything to lose. I figure you'd probably try almost anything. I would do the same in your position."

"I'm not sure I follow you."

She shrugged, pursed her lips, and kept looking at me.

"Uh, by the way, what's your full name?" I asked, changing the subject. "Or do I call you Nurse Lois?"

"No, you don't. The last name is Darnid. Like 'Darn it' with a 'd' on the end. Clang any gongs in your head?"

"Maybe a small one, Darnid," I said.

"It's *Doctor* Darnid—but you've always called me 'Lo.'"

"I thought you were a nurse."

"In all the psychological glory the Army boys could muster, they concluded that this nurse get-up would be less intimidating to you, more attractive," she said. "You've never liked medical doctors. Perhaps you recall that."

"Not really."

She glanced down at her uniform and then, looking straight into my eyes, mischievously undid the top button. It wasn't enough to show me much, but it had an effect.

My tongue felt ridiculously dry.

"Were they right?" she asked, undoing the next button. "About me being more attractive?"

I swallowed hard, looked at her full figure with admiration, and admitted, "Yeah, they were. In spades. But why would they care?"

She didn't unfasten any more buttons.

She dropped her eyes, let her hands fall to her sides, and said, "They were hoping it would be therapeutic, because you and I were—" she broke off and covered her mouth, turning slightly away, but not before I saw a tear run down her cheek.

"What the—?" I said, bewildered by the mood flip.

I automatically reached out to her and when I touched her hand, she all but fell into my arms. We sprawled awkwardly, half lying and half sitting on the bed together. It wasn't exactly comfortable, but awkward moments usually aren't. I made the best of it as she let her tears flood, punctuated by waves of sobs. I uttered what comfort I could, but to her credit, it didn't take her long to pull it together. *That* clanged a memory gong. Lo had never been much for extended emotional indulgences. It was something I'd always respected.

She sat up slowly, groaned, grabbed a tissue out of the box near the bed, blew her nose twice, and then turned purposefully toward me.

"Eddie," she said. "Do you *really* not remember what we were to each other?"

"Dan has hinted that we were a minor item. But he hasn't exactly encouraged me to pursue anything with you. I have the impression he wants me to think it was more you who was interested than me."

"A minor *item*? Sounds like a spare part for a car."

"Hey, I didn't mean—"

"Oh, never mind. Look at this," she said, reaching into her pocket. "Hold out your hand, Mr. Megabrain."

I hesitated a moment, then did it. She dropped something small and heavy into my palm. It was a gold ring.

"That," she said, "is the engagement ring you gave me the day before they stuck you into that skull-scrubbing machine."

I looked back and forth between her and the ring several times, trying to remember.

"Lo, I'm sorry. It doesn't fish anything out of the well."

"Maybe this will," she said, gently cupping my face in her hands and giving me a long, tender kiss.

If I was the frog-prince, she was the real princess.

It *did* bring things back—slowly at first, and then with a surge of images and emotions—dates we'd had, kisses and snuggles, video movies and popcorn, a classical music concert, an art gallery tour, long discussions about any and everything, and finally, my presenting her with the ring and asking her to marry me. And her saying yes.

"Well," I whispered hoarsely, "apparently I'm still in love

with you."

The tears came again as she nodded, "Yes, damn it, you sure apparently are!"

She pushed me onto my back and kissed me again, longer this time. I tasted tears on her lips.

After a minute or so, I had to come up for air. I sat up and so did she, her eyes dreamy.

"I just remembered something else, Lo. Our vow. The not-'til-we're-married one. I promised you that, didn't I?"

She shook her head, laughed softly, and nodded, her dark hair bobbing. "Yes, yes, you did! God, Eddie, it's good to have you back!"

She smiled at me with those startling, cobalt blue eyes, gave me a quick kiss, got up, straightened her uniform self-consciously, and said, "I intend to see that we keep that vow. I know celibacy is old-fashioned here in the 21st century, but—"

"It's a matter of honor," I finished.

I'd heard her say it a dozen times, usually related to an event such as my hands wandering toward forbidden places.

"I think it's fine, Lo, really."

She smiled teasingly, "Fine, but frustrating, huh?"

"Well—I won't deny it. Hey, I'm a natural man," I said, indicating a prominent protrusion under my hospital gown.

"That you seem to be," she said, closing the two buttons on her uniform. She sighed. "At least you are when it comes to bedroom thoughts."

"I detect an undercurrent of the unspoken," I said.

She sat on the edge of the bed in a no-monkey-business posture. There would be no further spontaneous wrestling.

She patted my hand chastely, and said, "Not exactly."

"Not exactly what?"

"A natural man. You're not. You know that. They've explained it to you, and as far as they went, they didn't exaggerate. Upstairs, Eddie, you truly are something unique. I think General Jefferson is right. The Lord is trying something new on this planet, and you're it."

"You sound serious."

"I was. I am." Taking both my hands she said urgently, "Listen to me, Eddie. I've disabled the monitoring station into this room for about another fifteen minutes. It's running a digital recording of you sleeping last night when I was in here checking on you. They know I'm in here, but they don't know we're talking."

"One of the perks of being both the med-chief and experienced in security apparatus," I noted, recalling more of her background, which was amazingly varied.

"Yes, exactly. Pay attention, Eddie. I've got something to tell you that no one else on this base should hear, and I don't have long."

"Shoot," I said, my attitude sobering up as I saw the stern look that clouded her face.

"Eddie, they're not planning on letting you out of here. Ever. There won't be a meeting tomorrow morning. That was a ruse to lull you. They're going to put you back under the MI tonight, after you fall asleep. Oh, they'll feed you pleasant dreams and keep you reasonably healthy. But you'll never wake up again. Anyway, not for a long, long time. Not if they can help it."

"Humph," I snorted. "I suppose that should surprise me, but it doesn't. That's why I faked feeling bad. I could sense that something was up and wanted to get away. I had to give myself breathing room to mull the situation over, to let that warning light in the back of my brain add some detailed code to its message."

"You always had good intuition," Lo observed. "It's not just your logic circuits that run on warp drive."

"Yeah, well, despite what everyone says about my mental capacities, thinking still requires time and I do screw up. Right now, I don't feel like I can afford any."

I shifted my weight to stretch.

"However, I can't say that I understand what Dan's doing, Lo. Now there's a guy making a big mistake. Can't he see through Jefferson's shenanigans? I thought Dan had more of an ethical compass."

"Don't blame Dan too much, Eddie—and don't judge him on the basis of your exalted opinions gained under the MI virtual personality. He's not like that. Except for being a bit brighter than normal, in most ways Dan's an ordinary guy. Don't expect heroics from him. His hands are tied. He's a loyal soldier and has his orders. I'm afraid many of them have included deceiving you. It's Jefferson calling the shots. I seriously doubt that Dan will cross him. Oh, I'm not saying Dan likes this bitter stew. He doesn't. It tastes bad to him. He is—or was—your friend, although not as close as that MI program led you to believe. He likes you, but I don't think I'd count on his crawling through razor wire for you. Even so, the whole thing is abrading his conscience, like some kind of insidious emotional strep germ."

"He's in too deep to back out."

She nodded. "Tragic, but I know him. He's a nice guy when he's not under pressure, but he probably won't save you, Eddie. Maybe long ago he might have tried, but the years have shortened his honor. He's said 'yes' so many times that he's forgotten that 'no' is an option anymore. Only you can get yourself out of this mess, Eddie. And me, I hope. If I can help. Just tell me what to do."

"First explain to me what you meant about not being a natural woman."

"Oh, that. Well, I don't have your mental Slowdown capabilities, if that's what you're thinking. However, I didn't fall off the hay wagon last Tuesday, either. They tested me, and decided that I was about as close to your level as anyone might ever get. My I.Q. stands pretty tall, too."

"You don't have to justify your brains to me, Lo. It's obvious that you've got more than sand between your ears. I don't trust I.Q. tests, anyway. Did you know that those things were never originally intended as a measure of general adult intelligence? I'll take high doses of honesty, courage, ambition, and perseverance over the I.Q. lottery any day of the week."

"Well, whatever. *They* think I.Q. is important. But that's not the only thing they liked about me. You see, my genetic history is so healthy it would make you sick to look at the chart."

She ran a hand through her glossy brown hair, a gesture I'd seen often, and continued, "At first, before you allegedly went rogue and got squashed into that infernal MI machine, they'd encouraged our romance. I went along—as a duty."

"You were *ordered* to woo me?"

She nodded, looking down at her fingernails.

"They wanted us to have kids, sweetheart. They wanted to see if I could bake up big batches of hyper-speed mini-Eddies. You probably think I was awful for even considering such a thing under orders. However, you see, I know they're right about you. In the abstract, it makes sense to try to conserve whatever genes help make you what you are. Anyway, I used to think so. Then, after I got to know you, I somehow fell in love and— Well, that changed everything. Also, I started finding out more about the program, Project BTB, they call it."

"BTB?"

"Before the Beginning. That's the rumor. They picked the name after you went under the MI. You never knew about it. But I don't think anyone knows for sure what it stands for, except maybe Jefferson."

"Before, before . . . Hmm, not *B-4*, is it?"

"What's that?"

"Oh, a rumored, radically advanced stealth plane. Some people also call it The Plate. Jefferson's outfit was once said to be doing some work on its avionics. Naw, probably a coincidence."

"Some of the techies—who don't like the pressure Jefferson's put you through—say BTB stands for Break the Bastard. You being the bastard. You've never been exactly freely forthcoming with your compliance. You've always had the highly unmilitary gall to question virtually everything. That's why Jefferson decided to declare you a rogue."

"You're saying I actually wasn't?"

"Not in the way he and Dan told you. You never threatened to expose anything in here. Yes, you threw a couple tantrums, but you always took your oaths of secrecy seriously.

Not a black spot on your record until the good general got out his ink bottle. That's Jefferson's justification. Pulled it out of thin air with 'verification' statements from his lap dogs. They'll suck up anything he sticks their snouts in. Believe me, he's faked some convincing-looking evidence condemning you as a grave national security risk. He wants to keep you here at all costs. If he can declare you a major risk, he figures it'll be a lot easier to slap a leash around your neck and keep it there. He's got the discretionary power to do it."

"But why? Am I missing something here?"

She frowned and got out a little light that doctors use to look through your pupils.

"Uh-huh, thought so," she muttered, "you're head's still a bit fuzzed. Shows up as a slight macular swelling. Short-term memory doesn't come back all at once, either. Spotty. Should be better soon, though. The short-term retrieval returns fully before the long-term stuff snaps back into order. Your long-term is getting better fast, so I imagine the short-term problem will take care of itself any time."

She put the light away and said, "Jefferson and his boys think they can use you to start the human race over again on a new, higher plane."

I made a sour face and spat out an obscenity.

"I'm supposed to be their starter yeast. And what? You're supposed to be the hot little oven?"

"That *was* the idea, all right."

"Why does the concept feel like a great big slug crawling down my throat?"

"Probably because it ought to be our choice, not theirs. Probably because neither of us looks forward to being cattle in a human factory farm. Besides, there's more to it than that."

"I'm not sure I can take anymore."

"Well, you need to know. It wasn't just me they were going to use, Eddie. They've got a whole squad of women lined up to be inseminated and bake your babies. Jefferson's bragged about it. Personally screened them, I'm told."

"I'll bet."

"He's gotten so cocky that he's not quite as careful as he ought to be. Here's the butter on the bread, Eddie. He's decided that it would be better to have you unconscious in the MI machine, providing donor sperm for an endless line of experimental moms. No matter what he's led you to believe, he has no intention of *either* letting you off this base or remaining conscious. He'll pack you into that machine and feed you appropriately romantic virtual reality dreams and you'll be nothing more than a chained bull."

"What about you?"

"Me?" she said, rolling her eyes. "Oh, that. He's grown suspicious of me. See, he never wanted me to get emotionally close—only pretend to. He's got a respectable intuitive radar himself. I think he knows I'm against the whole deal, even though I've done my best to hide it. I knew if I didn't I'd have no chance of saving you. He's already given me transfer orders out of here, effective in a month. I'll be off to some igloo in Alaska digging ice blocks for the foreseeable future. He said it's either that or I can opt for a generous, but immediate retirement—and a stiff promise never to talk about any of this. He's been disgustingly polite about it, naturally. He doesn't dare tell me his true feelings."

I shook my head wearily. "God, Lo. I thought stuff like this had gone out with Hitler back in the middle of the last century. I never would have believed that our own military would—"

"Don't pound with too heavy a hammer, Eddie," Lo said sharply, holding up a palm. "It's *not* the whole military. I come from a military family and I respect the service. It's an honorable crowd, at least in this country. I doubt if 99.9% of the troops or brass would go for this project. Hell, a lot of people *here* don't go for it, though they only grumble among themselves. You want to talk about rogue? The real rogue is Jefferson. He's been granted so much discretionary authority over this cozy, isolated incubator base that he thinks he can do anything he wants. Worse, he thinks God is on his side."

I laughed.

"I'm serious."

"Well, I heard him quote the Bible, but that's no indictment of anyone."

"No it's not—and you don't have to point it out to me. I'm a believer myself. As you probably remember by now, it's always been a point of friendly dispute between us. You being a non-believer. You've got Ayn Rand and I've got God and we're probably going to argue about it 'til doomsday."

"I thought it was Dan who was the Rand fan. Oh, no. I see. The MI reversed it from me to him. Dirty trick. Okay, it's falling into place now."

I whacked my temple with the flat of my palm, "Geez! When is all this stuff going to straighten out, Lo!"

She squeezed my shoulder affectionately and said, "Give it time. You'll have it together before you know it. Unless God holds a grudge against atheists," she said, smirking.

"I don't call myself an atheist anymore. I've decided I'm a skeptical agnostic."

"Uh-huh. Whatever euphemism you want," she said, chuckling dryly, then fast getting serious again. "The point I was making was that Jefferson has mixed up his religion pretty thoroughly with his inflated ego. Get this. He's convinced himself he's God's personal conduit for cutting edge science."

"Could you be exaggerating a touch, Lo?"

I asked it, because a memory had sizzled to the forefront about Lo's tendency to overstatement under stress.

She shook her head and said, "Not this time; not on this matter. You've got to understand the scope of it. I've got a minor in history, Eddie, remember? Believe me, there have been plenty of stewballs like Jefferson over the years, in governments everywhere, and not just in the military. Once they get enough power, and hold onto it unchallenged too long, they start to feel *sacredly* inspired. Who's to tell them otherwise? Who's to bring them back down to earth? Once their power becomes almost absolute—as Jefferson's is over this installation—their sense of earthly perspective melts like an ice cube on a summer sidewalk. How do you think the Divine Right of Kings was justified, or for that matter any of the theocracies? Oh, I'm not saying everyone falls prey like he has. They don't. But a lot have. Man's history is strewn with the wreckage of their screwy schemes and utopianism.."

"Be that as it may, he's certainly the practical problem standing between me and my freedom."

"That he is. You don't have long to deal with him, either. A few hours at most."

She looked at her watch. "I've got to get back to my station, Eddie. Only a couple minutes to go."

She bent forward and kissed me long and hard, then said a bit breathlessly, "I meant it, you know. I'll help, in any way I can. Let me know if you get any good ideas."

As she moved reluctantly to the door, holding eye contact, I winked and said, "I already have."

She cocked her head and asked, "You have? What?"

"We've got to escape, of course — and forever disappear from the face of the earth."

Chapter 14

Her hand on the door, she said, "That's a heavy prescription, isn't it?"

"No. We can do it. We *have* to do it. Can you re-boot your video digital diversion and duck back in here in, say, an hour? Don't worry, Lo. I'm not going to be anyone's pet bull. Not even for the Biblical prize of going down in history as Adam Number Two."

I told her a few more things, causing her to smile brightly, blow me a kiss, and slip out the door.

I showered and shaved and tried to get my brain to slide into mental Slowdown. At first it wouldn't kick in, but I kept at it, breaking down the remnants of the MI wall, brick by mental brick. After a few minutes, the wall crumbled and I had the Slowdown back in full force. I sighed in relief. By the time Lo got back, I had a plan. Not without risk, but a plan, nevertheless.

"Okay," I said, after stealing a light kiss, "everything all right outside?"

She nodded and replied, "We've got about thirty minutes to talk, if you need that much time."

"It'll take less than half that. Here's what I've got in mind . . . "

Ten minutes later, Lo left briefly and returned with one of the plant security guards. She used the pretense that I was unconscious and she needed a hand to turn me over to give me a shot. The medical staff was always short on help, so this wasn't an unusual request. The security guards were frequently bored and welcomed a break in routine.

I stayed quiet with my eyes closed. He approached the bed with Lo, chatting amiably and trying to snatch a peek of her cleavage — which she'd encouraged by unfastening the top two buttons of her blouse and deliberately bending toward him. I opened my eyes slightly and went into Slowdown. The light underwent a slight shift to the red. I snaked a fist out and caught him hard under the jaw. He literally never saw it coming. I got out of bed and was behind him in time to catch him. Lo had shifted no more than a fraction of an inch. I was moving many times faster than either of them. If Lo saw me at all, I was nothing but a blur. I willed myself out of the Slowdown and the guard collapsed into my arms.

Lo looked at me in amazement and said, "I didn't see anything! What happened?"

I grinned cockily and said, "Jefferson and Dan were obviously wrong."

"About what?"

As I lifted the guard onto the bed, I said, "They thought I'd only inherited a mental Slowdown effect, not the physical one like my half-brother Kevin. I have both."

Lo's hand went to her mouth in astonishment.

"Oh, it's true," I assured her. "Always have had it — and I've always hidden it. Jefferson never found out because he thought the physical version could only work under sudden duress. That's how it is with Kevin, I guess, and his family. Jefferson never imagined that I could control it at will so he never found it. When he tried his tricky tests, I refused to activate the Slowdown. I didn't just out-think those thugs on the streets back in L.A. when I was a kid; I literally ran circles around them. They used to call me the Asphalt Ghost. They were afraid of me. I was always where I wasn't supposed to be and I could never be caught or cornered. It was a survivor's dream reputation. Anyway, I'm glad for it, Lo. Thinking is critical, but it only takes you so far in the world, no matter how smart you are. In this case, we're going to need speed and bruises, too. Let's go."

"God willing," she said.

"I'll trust reason," I said, flicking her pretty chin with my index finger.

"Well, can I keep God as a back-up plan?"

"Your choice. Oops, one second."

I tucked the guard into bed on his side, pulling the covers up over his ears. To the camera, when the system came back on live, he'd look like me. His hair was the same color and he was roughly my size.

"Let's blow this eugenics farm, Lo. In a few minutes, you'll 'wake up' and sound the alarm and scream holy murder. It's all up to me now. If this works—if they don't drag me back in within a few hours—you'll know I've made it. Then I'll have to bide my time before coming for you."

"When?"

I shook my head and said, "I don't know exactly. It depends on how closely they keep an eye on you. You might be a suspect, at least for awhile. As careful as you've been, you might have missed something."

"I don't think I did," she said. "They'll assume what it's logical to assume: that their super-genius out-thought them. Don't worry. I can handle myself if I know we'll eventually find each other. But don't take forever, okay? I want that ring you gave me to mean something."

I pulled her to me and kissed her in a way that left no doubts.

"I'll know when the time is right, Lo. Just stay out of that damned MI machine. It can be used for deep interrogation, too, you know."

She shuddered and said vehemently, "They'll have to drag me by my toenails to get me into that Devil's device. Besides, I've made plans, too."

"Eh?"

"If you recall, I've got considerable computer programming skills. I've got an idea for how to disable the MI for a long time. I plan to set loose a stealthy, self-regenerating virus that they won't be able to kill short of using a baseball bat."

I gave her a reassuring smile.

"I'm learning to trust your self-preservation drive, Lo."

"As well you should."

"Now, do you have that spare uniform and other stuff?"

"Right here."

She rapidly emptied the 'nurse' satchel that she always carried with her—actually a modified doctor's bag. Given the nature of their work, and the risk of being bloodied or otherwise splattered, all the medical personnel had spare uniforms in the dressing room, which was only a few doors away. Before luring in the guard, she'd stopped and picked out a male outfit; basically pants and a V-neck pullover cotton shirt. I quickly slid out of my gown, crumpled it and dumped it down the room's laundry chute.

"What about the ID badge?"

Lo reached into her pocket and produced one, explaining, "I liberated this. Don't ask how. It's an old one from a guy who used to work here. It won't pass muster close-up, but it should at a casual glance—"

"Right," I said, pinning it on. "I don't plan on sitting down for close-ups. Don't they have miniaturized ID transmitters in these things yet? They were scheduled to upgrade last year. That's what I recall before they mashed me into the MI."

"Only for the top brass, so far. Budgets, you know."

"Security," I swore, "the first to be cut, then the first to be blamed. You'd think they'd learn not to skimp."

"Well, thank God for you that they did in this case."

"Where'd you find this?" I asked, holding up a short, blonde wig—almost a butch cut.

"Sally, one of the night nurses I know. She keeps two or three in her locker. She likes variety. I'm afraid she's not terribly careful about keeping her door code secret. Did I mention that I've got an eidetic memory, too?"

"No, but I'm glad," I said, putting the wig on. "How do I look?"

"Not bad. The ID card picture is blonde. That's the idea."

She adjusted the piece to make sure none of my own, darker

hair showed, then momentarily put her hand on my cheek.

"Before you go," she said, "one last thing."

"Yeah?"

"Come back to me, Eddie."

She kissed me.

"I will," I said.

Then I smacked her nose hard with the flat of my hand. She staggered and began to bleed like a tipped wine glass.

She grinned through the blood as she let it run freely over her front. Nothing like a bad nose bleed to convince people that you were a victim of a crazy escapee. Especially if you were a woman.

"Yeah," I said, smiling. "That ought to do it."

Then I went into Slowdown. From her point of view, I simply disappeared. The Asphalt Ghost lived again.

The Slowdown isn't an unmitigated blessing. The problem with the physical version is twofold.

First, you have to learn a different way of moving. At the speeds involved, you can hurt yourself, or someone else, badly and easily. Speed equals energy. For instance, if you decide to pop a guard on the jaw while under the effect, you have to consciously control that specific action in order to avoid taking the guy's face off. The Slowdown comes with its own, internal compensation system. I've never investigated the details. Without it, I'd burn out my own body with only a few movements; or snap an arm or leg—or my neck. Inertia carries a bruising price, even internally.

Second, despite the inborn compensation factors, remarkable as they are, there's still a price. If I move continuously for too long, I can wear myself out for a week. Back on the streets of L.A., before I learned my limitations, I'd done it several times. I'd ended up as a basket case of aches and bruises.

That's why I'd developed my own strategy of compensation. I called it Toon Mode. Remember the old cartoons where the cat zipped from tree to tree, stopping at each one, as he stalked the bird? It's kind of like that. The trick is to use the Slowdown selectively, only for those stretches of motion when you absolutely need it. Otherwise, ordinary sneakiness suffices.

Nice theory. There was one problem with that inside the base. Security cameras covered most of the open areas in the facility. While they weren't constantly monitored by a live human, I could never know for sure when they were. That's why I needed the male nurse disguise. When I moved at normal speed through areas under watch, I needed to look like someone else, someone who, at a glance, belonged in this underground magic shop.

In fast speed, I dodged out the door and down into the maze of small buildings and cubicles. Normal exits were off-limits to me. Not only were they all camera-covered, but the codes were changed daily and were for all intents and purposes inviolable. I knew. I'd been a busy boy. In my earlier, pre-MI life, I'd helped design the security system. I doubted that they'd changed it much. What I needed was a more circumspect way out.

Alternately dodging in fast mode and strolling casually in normal mode, I made my way to the maintenance building. Logic said that there were probably unmarked exits from the base, because without them, proper maintenance would have been almost impossible. Everything—whether computer programs or industrial plants or bases—had ways in and out that were unusual and known to only a few people.

A quick reconnoiter inside the building determined that there were two people inside, beefy looking fellows in helmets working on a welding project in the back. In a cubicle near the middle of the building, I found a computer work station. It was out of sight of the two workers and of surveillance.

I went into mental Slowdown again. It is great for computer work. In a few seconds of hacking I located the basic schematic of the ducts, shafts, by-ways, half-floors, and other passageways and access channels for the various systems needed to keep an underground base like this operating smoothly. Caves within caves, I thought.

It took another several seconds to find the chart of the unmarked exits. All three of the normal exits were either elevators or straight inclines, man-made passages to the base surface. No-nonsense, pour-the-concrete mentality. Two exits were for personnel and one was for cargo. I didn't want any of those.

The unmarked exits, as I'd suspected, opened into the Darkhorse cave system. There were several. Four went into a section of the caves I didn't know about, down on the back of the hill, but the fifth opened up near the howler geyser. The geyser was a part of the power-plant's venting plan, so it made sense that someone would want an easy way to get at it in case something needed to be cleaned or fixed.

I committed the routes to memory, jumped into the security system and ordered it to unlock the critical doors along my way for a period of fifteen minutes, and then told the master computer to wipe its log of my illegal access. That finished, I checked to see if there was anyone new in the building—and almost slammed into a guy walking past the computer cubicle.

"Hey!" he shouted. "Oh, sorry, nurse."

"That's okay," I said gruffly. I brushed past him and said, "Just looking for Jack. We had an appointment. Guess I must've missed him."

"Who?" he asked.

"Maybe it was Joe," I said over my shoulder and walked out of sight around a hallway bend.

"Joe?" I heard him shout, uncertainly. "Wait a minute there, buddy!"

I glanced over my shoulder and saw him move toward me.

Great. Just what I needed. A civic-minded maintenance man.

Well, there was a way to handle that. As I rounded a second bend, I shifted into full Slowdown mode and headed out of maintenance toward the power plant. I dodged by three people, who, from my point of view were standing still. To them, I was a corner-of-the-eye fog that didn't consciously register in their vision.

The point of entry to the maintenance tunnel that led to the howler was near the power plant, but the door was outside the main structure, hidden in a sidewall behind a couple of garbage bins. That's where I crouched and caught my breath for about a minute. Normally, short Slowdown bursts like that didn't bother me much. But I'd been under the MI for two years, and despite electrical stimulation of muscles and supplement-induced boosters, I'd lost some stamina. That red light in my brain was blinking again, too. So far, so good it was telling me—but watch out! Trouble was, I didn't know what it sensed that my conscious mind did not. I peeked in all directions and saw nothing. I listened and heard nothing. I even tried sniffing, but smelled nothing. Finally, I shrugged and tried the door.

It was unlocked, as it was supposed to be according to the instructions I'd given the computer. It squeaked as if it hadn't been used in awhile. I moved in and closed it behind me. The passageway before me was dimly lit and lined with ducts and piping and electrical cables on the left side. It was smooth-walled, green-painted concrete on the right. The passage headed down at about a seven-degree angle. There was no point wasting energy on the Slowdown here. According to the schematics, there weren't any active security cameras in these tunnels anymore. Oh, cameras were there, all right. I spotted one about every forty or fifty feet. Although they were nearly state-of-the art—Sony 7200 dpi full-color ultra-CCDs—according to the logs, they'd been tagged "disabled" in the base's security program. I was grateful, but abstractly I disapproved. In a place like this, *every* entrance or exit should have been priority watched, down the throat and up the ass. Sounded good in concept. In practice, however, budgets often severely limited military security. The "nobody'd ever try to go *there!*" mentality was also a factor—an attitude that tended to drive security bosses nuts.

I glanced at my watch. More time had passed than I'd figured. If I didn't get out of the caves soon, I never would. Oh, well, I thought, tripping into physical Slowdown, live now and pay later or die trying.

I became a haze of motion down the tunnel through several twists and turns, finally coming to a corridor with a door at the far end. I dropped out of fast speed and looked it over. Yes, it was the one that was supposed to open in a hidden nook in the corner of the "howler" room. I pushed it. Instead of opening, as it was supposed to, it refused to budge. I shoved harder. I ramped back into quick-time and slammed it. It didn't give an inch. I stopped and considered. Unless my memory was playing tricks on me again, I knew I'd ordered the computer to unlock this exit. I bent close and looked at the seam of the lock in the light. I could see the magnetic deadbolt crossing into the wall.

"Looks like you're stuck, ol' bud," Dan's bass voice said behind me.

I whirled and blurted, "What the — "

Dan had his service automatic trained on me.

"You're far from the only one who can think ahead, Eddie. I figured you'd scoot this way. What *you* didn't figure was that there was a shorter way here. If you'd checked the maintenance construction addendum files, and not just the main ones, you'd have known that there was a new corridor in this section, one designed to carry a cart. It shortcuts several minutes off your route. Plus, you didn't figure that someone might stumble onto Lois soon after you smacked her."

"You?"

"Jefferson and me both, as a matter of fact. He stopped by and wanted to see how you were doing. Asset-checking, he called it. When we found Lois bleeding all over creation and saw the mashed up guard lying unconscious, Jefferson hit the roof and ordered a base-wide, quiet alert. That's why you didn't hear any sirens or bells, in case you were wondering. Then Jefferson took off to round up a security squad and I headed here. Given the head start I had, even with your physical Slow-down skills — which I think I just glimpsed — you couldn't beat me here."

He kicked the side of the corridor and a door I hadn't noticed swung into the new access passage he'd mentioned. A golf-cart-looking vehicle stood there.

"How'd you guess I'd head this way?" I asked.

"Logical choice. Everything else was either monitored or unfamiliar. I figured the howler would seem like friendly territory. Besides, I'm a poker buddy with one of the maintenance guys. I remembered that he'd mentioned this access was dis-abled. Something went wrong with the magnetic lock over a year ago and no one got around to fixing it. Hardly ever used, so they settled for opening it manually. All these maintenance doors have manual overrides—but you have to have a key. You don't have one."

"No," I said. I nodded toward the gun, "So this is it, I guess."

"Yeah, I'm afraid so," Dan said. Then he grinned slowly, reached into his pocket, and pulled out a key. He flipped it to me. "Get the hell out of here, ol' bud. While there's still time. I'll beat it back before anyone figures I've been down here to help you. *None* of the security cameras are on down here any-more. I know."

I looked at him with my jaw hanging down to my belt.

"You look pretty stupid, you know," he said. "Get going, before what little honor I've got left crawls back into the hole it usually lives in these days."

He held out his right hand. We shook. His hand was trem-bling slightly.

"I'll never forget this, Dan," I said.

"If you're smart, you will. Disappear, Eddie. Do it well. Because Jefferson is obsessed. He'll hunt you and never give up. If he catches you, he'll bury you so deep in the MI world that you'll never see reality again. Go, damn you!"

He spun on his heel and walked through into the new cor-ridor, slamming its door shut behind him. I heard the electric whine of the cart start up and move away.

I stuck the key in the lock and opened the door to the howler room. The geyser was dormant at the moment. I locked the door behind me and dropped the key down the howler hole. That would take awhile to find.

Then I went into Slowdown and sped out of the caves of Darkhorse for real.

By the time the helicopters got organized and came over Darkhorse Butte twenty minutes later, looking for me, I was out of the area entirely. I paid a heavy price. I had to use the Slowdown almost continuously for several hours to get as far away from the base as I possibly could. It took me a month to recover completely.

Chapter 15

So, here I am, in another city, finishing this amateur recording of my story.

Looking back, I can see that Jefferson not only missed my physical Slowdown effect, but he clearly didn't figure me for retaining as much of my roguish streak. Not roguish in criminal terms, no. Rather, it was in terms of having a strong sense of my own self-interest. He made a general's classical error: underestimating the enemy. Maybe he'd been able to squelch rebellion in earlier subjects of MI programming, but he hadn't succeeded with me. Why? Maybe the mental Slowdown has some built-in self-preservation reaction. Or maybe I was just lucky. I don't know.

But I'd had enough of being a hyper-gopher with a jacked-up brain. Look where it had led me. Indirectly, at least, I was responsible for the Engels Extension conflict, for World War 3, for God's sake!

I can see now that I should have built in some kind of self-destruct safeguards on the antimatter weapons specs. I think I could have done it. If I had, then when the Rooskies stole the specs, they'd not have been able to make much of them. Perhaps, perhaps not. They have their geniuses over there, too. I could have at least tried. I was smart enough to have anticipated it and tried, yet I hadn't. There were probably a half-dozen things I could have done. I saw the war *and* the theft of the antimatter gun specs coming. I'd forecast it. I should have relied on my own judgment and acted. I won't make that kind of mistake again.

Right now, I feel as though I'm an eagle that's been asleep for a long time, finally starting to spread its wings again. From the depths of the caves to the heights of the skies, there is much before me. I feel *free* for the first time in my life. I want to find out what Eddie Jones could be if he were to put all of his mind and physical prowess to work. I want to lead *my* life the way I want for a change. I want to live unashamed and unconstrained and unbound by someone else's idea of what my course ought to be. What will I do? What will I become? I don't know yet. There's so much to explore before I can decide.

Am I a new Adam—a kind of John Galt of the next stage of evolution? Well, if I am, then how do I go about starting a new world? Tall order! What strategy and tactics do I use? And is it purely *my* business? If what Jefferson and Dan said is true, if my mind is an evolutionary leap, if I'm the first in a new species to succeed and eventually supersede mankind, then do I have a natural right to operate by my own rules? What are my constraints? What do I owe humanity? What are my moral limitations, if any? How do I determine them? Are conventional ethics relevant to me?

Oh, and does Lo really want to become my Eve? Sure, she loves me, and it's gotten stronger since I snatched her off that gloomy base up in Alaska. But does she truly know what she's getting into if we start down that road? Is it even possible? Am I perhaps an evolutionary dead-end—a human mule? Some questions don't come easy, even for a hyper-genius.

And what about the strange metal ring in the caves? Is there something else, another weird project, going on that they kept from me? How were the Russians involved? Or was that only part of the MI machine's fantasy world?

There's a hell of a lot to mull over. I guess if anyone is equipped to find the answers, it's me. Or so they say.

Well, ask me in five years. What will I be like in five years? A back of the envelope calculation tells me that I may accomplish what would take a normal man fifty years to achieve. If all the tests are right, that's the scale of difference. It has a hell of a lot of implications.

I don't plan on leaving an easy trail, not for anyone. Dan was right that Jefferson will never give up. He's got God and the Divine Right of Meddling on his side and if there's going to be a new race, he wants to run it. In some men, conceit knows no borders.

I'll be around, though, operating on the edge of things, out of sight, the Asphalt Ghost watching and deciding—with lovely Lo at my side, now and then kicking my shins to make me look where my feet are stepping.

Yes, ask—if you can find us. But unless we decide to let you, don't count on it.

By "you," I mean mankind, because I leave this fresh recording to all of you. Multiple copies are going out to the media and many others in this country and abroad. Way too many copies for General Jefferson and his henchmen to intercept and suppress.

Don't believe any of it? Some? All? It's up to you. Make of it what you will.

Just don't forget: *everything* has a reason.

Enough said.

I have a future to create.

AUTHOR'S DISCLAIMER:

The location of this story, the small city of Lebanon, Oregon, actually exists. It is one of the oldest towns in the West. There is a Horse Butte nearby. I spent many hours in my youth exploring it. However, there is no Darkhorse Butte. Nor is there a secret military base behind it or underneath it. There is no massive cave system haunted by a demon. Of course, I wouldn't check it out alone — or at night.

About the Author:

E. G. Ross lives near Eugene, Oregon. A military and foreign affairs writer for 30 years, Ross edits the Internet daily www.ObjectiveAmerican.com *and the monthly worldwide newsletter* The Objective American. *For fifteen years, he has operated Understanding Defense Research, a private institute that analyzes strategic and defense issues.*

Sneak Preview . . .

An All-New Technothriller
coming soon from
Premiere Editions International, Inc.

THE OREGON REBELLION
by E. G. ROSS

Prologue

"What's going on?" the sergeant yelled into the dented, dirt-crusted radio. "Son, I want you to talk to me!"

There was a short pause and a click. Then the young private's voice hissed in an urgent, rushing whisper, peppered with digital breakup, barely comprehensible, "Sir, they're . . . the match to the butt of the nuke . . . gonna fry the *capital* . . . Sir, what do I . . . can't squat here like a . . . is down and bleedin' . . . don't know if I can get to her and make—"

"Take it easy, soldier," the sergeant soothed. "Your mission is to cock and rock your monster gun. We're on your trail. Stay *cool*, son, or you'll bust us open like a rotten pumpkin!"

"Yes, sir!"

Face deeply lined with the strain of responsibility, the sergeant turned to his corporal. "I think he got that. I hope. Okay, listen up. In one minute you and I push in with Alpha, right behind our wonder boy. Let's hope he gets lucky with that high-tech popgun. Set the others to flank. We'll be rollin' smokes on the run."

The corporal frowned, "Sir, if I understood what I just heard, shouldn't we try to notify the capital to evacuate?"

The sergeant snorted and spat to one side. "Nuclear civil defense has been dead for decades. The civvies would have no idea how to scramble or where to ramble. We sure as *hell* can't teach 'em in an hour. Now haul ass!"

"Yes, sir!"

The corporal slid down the slight rise and slogged away over the marshy ground to carry out his orders. A chilling trickle of sweat ran down his spine as he muttered to himself, "How the hell could this be happening? How did it come to this? How in God's name did things get away from everyone, everywhere so damned *fast*?"

PART ONE: "Breakout"

Chapter 1:
"The GIRA Disease"

State Senate President J.B. Washington loosened his maroon tie. Sweat stung his eyes. He wiped it away with a crumpled white handkerchief. The air conditioning in the senate chambers was out. Again. The janitorial union's strike had seen to that. The temperature of the early August morning was edging past ninety. The forecast called for a high near 105, exceptionally warm for Salem, Oregon.

Tempers were riding the heat. For nine sweltering weeks J.B. and his "honorable" colleagues had argued. And argued. And argued some more. It was mind-numbing. The whole political fracas was about a single item: what to do about the lingering Oregon recession. Unemployment in June had topped an unheard of 18%. The state's residents were screaming. They wanted relief and they wanted it now.

Of course, the other states and the federal government were mired in their own economic *and* foreign problems. The malaise was nationwide, no doubt about that. Uncle Sam not only had no financial help to offer Oregon, but had recently implemented a stiff 10% national sales surtax. It was hitting most of the states hard, but Oregon especially so. Oregon was a proud state with a tough, independent pioneer tradition. This new federal burden seemed callous.

What had his wife Julie called it? "An indifferent elbow to

the jaw." That was about it, J.B. thought. He ground sweat out of his eyes with his thumb knuckles and sighed.

Not that the feds would budge on Oregon's account. They had a ready-made excuse: the U.S. Constitution didn't permit discriminatory taxation. If the rest of the nation had to suffer the new tax, well, too bad that Oregon's economy was among the least able to handle it.

J.B. swore inaudibly, "We're like a house cat trying to swallow a deer."

He reached under his desk and pulled a Coke out of the small fridge. He cracked it open with a practiced movement. It was his latest vice. He took a long swig while secretly wishing for a cigarette instead. Six months ago he'd assured Julie that he'd quit for good. But lately he'd been sneaking in three or four a day. He felt guilty, but consoled himself by giving silent credit to her observation at breakfast that morning. She'd nailed it. If Oregon was to recover soon from its first and worst recession of the early 21st century, it was going to have to nurse itself back to health. But with exactly what medicine?

He squinted across the haze of the chamber, watching his colleagues sweat and bicker. Bless Julie's helpful heart, but diagnosis was only half the answer. These doctors of democracy weren't stupid. But probably too good-willed by half. In J.B.'s opinion, it was their generosity that had let them fall prey to GIRA: Good Intentions Run Amok. The state taxes that had built up over the years were always for a "noble purpose." The regulations were always for "the public good." All the motives were pure-hearted and wonderful. The best altruism Oregon tax money could buy. But now, he mused, shaking his head, with years of nobility and goodness piled on a scale, the weight of the accumulated cost was outlandish. Worse, voters were using a lot of "or else" language. He shuddered. It was hard to believe, but two legislators had been attacked and beaten by mobs in their home towns. It was unheard of in easy-going Oregon. Five years ago, he could not have imagined it would come to this. Not in his craziest, most catastrophist daydreams.

Also by **E. G. ROSS . . .**

ENGELS
EXTENSION

It's the ultimate military threat. Diplomats and politicians consider it unthinkable. Yet out of the turmoil of Russia, a new and more virulent Soviet Union unexpectedly arises — with an arsenal of secret weapons immensely superior to nuclear bombs and precision missiles.

The poorly prepared, but courageous, American president has a chance to stop the new Soviets from imposing their old strategic obsession with world domination. Is there time? Or has America been fatally trapped by the Engels Extension?

Drawing on little-known technical and strategic trends, international defense writer E.G. Ross thrusts you into a tomorrow where the unthinkable becomes creepily real.

ISBN 0-9633818-6-5